Silent Night
THEME PARK
The Phantom Chasers

Edited by: ProofsbyPolly

Paperback ISBN: 978-1-990675-63-8

CONTENT WARNING

THIS NOVELLA CONTAINS THE FOLLOWING:
BLOOD
MURDER
GHOST RAPE
SEXUAL DEGRADATION
EXPLICIT SEX SCENES
BROTHER ON BROTHER
POSSESSION

IF YOU ARE SENSITIVE TO ANY OF THE
ABOVE CONTENT, PLEASE DO NOT
CONTINUE.

READER'S DISCRETION IS ADVISED

PROLOGUE

<u>**Silent Night Theme Park - A vacation resort for families**</u>
<u>**1976**</u>

Jeffrey wipes the sweat from his brow as he cranks the handle to start the ride. Why someone decided to put a Christmas theme park on an obscure island in the Florida Keys is beyond me. There's nothing Christmas-y about this place, except for the pervy Santas who are checking out the teenagers and the faux-snow-covered village homes.

"This thing's stuck again," Jeff groans out as he hauls once more on the crank, his back rippling with the effort.

I look up at the ride in question, a large circular structure with swings hanging from chains. This ride gives us the most trouble here at Silent Night, and no one knows what exactly is wrong with it.

"Maybe you didn't distribute the riders evenly," I suggest.

"Daniel," he snaps, his temper nearing its end. "I know how to work the fucking ride. I just want this fucking day to be over so I can go hang out with Moira."

Jeff is a pale-skinned redhead, but since he's been working here the last few weeks, he's been looking like a lobster from the hot Florida sun.

"Why don't you head on out? I can take it from here," I offer. "If I can't get it going, I'll get everyone off and shut it down for maintenance."

"I hate this place." Jeff wipes at his burned and blistering forehead again. "It feels like it's cursed."

He's not wrong. Getting this place up and running was a fucking nightmare, and most of the people working the rides are young adults with little to no theme park experience. Hence why we barely make minimum wage to deal with bullshit.

"You've had a long day," I coax. "I got this."

He steps back from the machine with a huff, his irritation hanging heavily over his head. His face is beet red as he gives me a firm nod, making his orange hair flop down over his forehead.

"Thanks, Danny," he mumbles. "I'll see you later tonight at the mess hall."

We all live here on the island while the theme park is open, all the way from November first until January thirty-first. We occupy the staff cabins on the other side of the island and convene for dinner in the mess hall each night. It's not a bad gig, but I miss my girlfriend back home, and my little sister, Christine.

"Hey, buddy," a man calls from his seat on the ride. "Are we moving or what?"

His attitude is pissing me off, and suddenly I understand why Jeff gets so fucking heated on top of the burning sun.

"Yeah, *buddy*!" I bite back and kick my foot out, ramming it into the crank.

It moves with a loud screeching noise, then the ride begins to spin as the eerie, fast-paced music starts up. I cross my arms over my chest and lean against the metal fencing surrounding the ride, feeling satisfied with myself when a gust of wind hits the back of my head.

Screams sound out as I spin around and watch, to my horror, as the ride spins at an ungodly speed. The swings are spinning straight out, putting pressure on the chains holding them.

I grab onto the crank and with all my might, yank it back, only to have it crack off in my hands. That's when the scraping sounds, like nails on a chalkboard, overpowering the high-pitched shrills.

Just when I thought it couldn't get any worse, the chains start to snap, one after another, and chairs fly through the air like catapults. I stand transfixed on the scene in front of me; the horror unfolding like a terrible nightmare.

"Danny!" I turn at the sound of my name, but something hits my throat, the force knocking the breath from my lungs.

I reach up and wrap my hand around it and feel warm liquid pouring through my fingers. With shock, I hold my hand out in front of me and drop to my knees when I see the bright red of my blood.

Jeff was right. This place is cursed.

ONE

Mary

<u>**Present Day**</u>

The dock creaks as I step out of the boat; the boards looking old and weathered. I wrap my arms around my waist as the wind kicks up and blows my curls in front of my face. It's a warm day, but a chill settles into my bones, giving the place an authentic Christmas feel.

Do I feel a similar energy here as I did at Belgrove? No.

I'm not being pulled to enter the grounds as if a tether has slipped between my ribs and settled around my heart, but I do feel something ominous. Terrible things happened here, and it's only a matter of time before James gives us all the gory details.

I will admit, this time I didn't do any research. With the echoing remnants of Belgrove still coursing through me, it was too hard to face the horror of this place. Another set of chains, rusted and eroded, are wrapped through a looming, industrial steel fence, and I look over my shoulder to find Connor standing there, his eyes sparkling with glee.

"I've never been to a theme park before," he says, his mouth climbing with a childlike grin.

"We went to Universal Studios the year we graduated from high school." I remind him as my forehead crumples with concern. Connor has not been himself since we left Belgrove, and as much as I understand that we all cope with trauma differently, he's recovered quite fast. He's even been more jovial than ever, which has been uncomfortable at some points, considering the rest of us have had trouble being happy at all.

"Right." He nods, keeping his eyes straight ahead, the wide grin still lining his mouth.

"Let's walk up together," Nick suggests as he stands next to Connor, grabbing his hand.

In one swift motion, Connor shakes Nick's hand from his own, without a single glance at him, and says, "Let's not be a bunch of girls."

Connor runs hot and cold these days, and we've all chalked it up to him dealing with what we've been through, but I can see how much it affects Nick. His shoulders immediately deflate as his eyes linger on their unclasped hands. I just want to wrap him in my arms and soothe away the rejection.

Heat hits my back and I have to bite my bottom lip when I smell musk and citrus. James' breath coats over my neck as he leans down to whisper, "Are you okay?" As much as he and I have been getting comfortable in our relationship, it's still a bit awkward for me around the others. We haven't taken the time to explore that yet.

I nod, not trusting my voice at the moment, making him chuckle. He knows exactly what kind of effect he has on me. Where I'm still treading in fresh waters with Nick and Connor, James and I have no issues with our relationship. It's a weird dynamic when your boyfriend is happy to share you with his two best friends, who are also seeing each other.

Thankfully, we don't care how it's perceived, because we only have each other in this world, no one else matters.

"I think we should walk up together," James reiterates, clasping his brother on the shoulder just as Jane barks from the boat. "We need Scooby too." James turns to laugh at the mangy dog. Jane jumps out of the boat and trots over to Connor, her scrawny tail wagging happily. She seems to be taken with him the most, although he doesn't show her much affection. It's an odd pairing. We all begin to walk up to the fence, seeing the path on the other side lined with broken and faded candy canes and completely overgrown with weeds. "They have cabins here," James begins. "The staff would live here while the theme park was open."

"Beats having to boat the hour back to the mainland," Connor says while Nick hums his agreement as he tries his best to suppress the disappointment, but I can see it in his eyes.

James pulls out the bolt cutters and breaks the chain off the fence. This time, there were no owners to talk to about visiting this place. It was abandoned after its first week of the grand opening and the tragedy that ensued. The company which funded and built the theme park had claimed bankruptcy, leaving this place to rot while waiting on someone to buy it.

Nick shoves open the gate as Connor and Jane saunter inside, both without a single care, but we three remain just outside the gates, our bodies stiff with tension.

"Are we really doing this again?" I whisper.

"The money is good," Nick mumbles.

"And we need the money," James adds. They each grab a hold of my hands, both squeezing in assurance as we watch Connor slowly disappear inside the theme park. "The first thing inside is Santa's workshop. It's a gift shop and restaurant in one," James informs us, his voice low and filled with trepidation. "Beyond that are the games and rides, and the scene of the most horrific theme park accident in history."

"It's just one night," Nick says with a nod, his sweaty palm betraying his fear.

"Famous last words," I groan out as we finally step through the gates.

Nick

The last time I willingly walked my ass into a haunted location, I was picked on by a ghost kid and bullied by a poltergeist. Sprinkle in a few traumatic orgasms and bam! That was Belgrove in a quick review.

Taking a look around me, I should be thankful it's not riddled with clowns, but then I spot a rusted sign with arrows pointing in the directions of certain locations around the park with a demonic-looking elf on it. Those things are supposed to be cheerful and spread joy, but the only thing this little shit is doing is spreading the creep right into my boxers.

I wouldn't say I've ever been one that actively shits his pants when dealing with the dead, but after Belgrove I know to always bring extra underpants. I give Mary's hand another squeeze, more for me than for her, and try to find where Connor walked off to.

Things between us have been rocky at best since Belgrove. A few stolen kisses here and there, but mainly shoves and yelling at me to get the fuck away from him. I know everyone deals with their trauma differently, but I can't help but feel like he's changed his entire outlook on being with me as my boyfriend. I can honestly say I love him and it's killing me seeing him pull away from me day after day.

"Hey, you, let's check out that gift shop and let James freak us out with the backstory of this place. What do you say?" Mary asks gently, pulling me from my inner sorrow. I didn't realize I was planted in one spot, lost in thought. Mary gives my hand a little tug, and I notice James watching me with concern. Both of them are patient and give me the minute I need.

Jane even brushes up against my leg in silent support, having left Connor to come back around to check on the rest of us. The mutt took some time to get used to us, but she's quickly grown into a part of our crew. I kneel, still holding onto Mary's hand, and scratch behind her ears, smiling when she gives a happy yip before trotting off. I stand and look back at Mary.

Before giving her a nod, I take a deep inhale and exhale. She smiles softly and we start on our way again. That easy little grin from her helps heal the wound Connor's left in me.

James releases Mary's hand as we arrive at Santa's workshop to shove open the warped door. The place isn't really dusty in this humidity, more moldy and slimy, and I watch as James' face screws up as he dusts his hands off. Mary releases my hand to go browse around and for one fleeting moment, I almost have a panic attack without her hand there to ground me. I focus on my breathing like James told me to do after we left Belgrove and wait for my racing heart to calm before I follow her lead to check out the shop.

A wall lined with mugs catches my attention. These folks in the south really like seeing their names on them. I start my hopeless search to see if maybe there's a reindeer mug with my name when the sound of shattering glass has me jolting upright and twisting around in search of my brother and Mary.

James is looking at a smashed ballerina figurine on the ground with his phone out recording. We decided for this investigation we'd film footage outside of being on the live stream since we had so many issues at Belgrove and that was one of the main viewer complaints. I nearly trip over Jane in one of the aisles, who has found a really old-ass doll to chew on as she tears through the shop with excitement.

"Activity?" I ask, feeling both parts excited and terrified as I put my focus back on James. Belgrove really did some damage to me. I'm starting to think we did this too soon before we were healed from the wounds inflicted on our souls. The money, however, can motivate the weakest into anything.

"No, that was me bumping into the table. Just getting a little footage for now before we go live," James replies with an apology in his eyes, like he knows I'm easily on edge right now.

I take a deep breath, letting my eyes flutter shut for a moment, and try my best to get my shit together when I feel arms wrap around me and a breath of air hits the back of my neck.

"I won't let anything happen to you. I can protect you," Connor says, shocking the fuck out of me. He found me before I could find him and I can only stand here, stunned stupid because this is the most affection I've gotten from him since Belgrove when our roles were reversed and I was his protector. My, how the tables have turned.

"You're hugging me willingly," I comment almost thoughtlessly. He squeezes me a moment longer, setting off all kinds of butterflies in my stomach before I feel the change come over him.

"Yeah, well, don't get used to it." He gives me a slight shove when he releases me, kind of like guys do when they're just buddies. I can most definitely NOT put him in the buddy category when I've had his dick down the back of my throat. Mary gives me a pitying look and rage fills me. I'm glad Connor enjoyed using me as his experiment with men, even though it was at the expense of my fucking heart.

"And we are going live in five, four, three, two," James says, breaking the mounting tension before holding up one digit in the air, signaling the start of the live stream. "Phantom Hood! How's it going? We are now live on Silent Night Theme Park Island, where the worst tragedy of any theme park has ever occurred. We just arrived on the island shortly ago, but I wanted to give you all an inside look at where we are setting up our headquarters for this investigation and give you all the history behind this place." James speaks animatedly into his phone.

While I know Belgrove did a number on him as well, he's always been a lot better at hiding it than the rest of us. I take a moment to browse around some more while I listen to him speak and ignore everyone else because I need a minute to chill before I do something stupid like punch Connor in his beautiful face for making me fall in love with a lie.

"When Silent Night was first being built, the contractors ran into so many issues with the setup. At first, it was minor things as simple as rides not being built to standard because of missing or broken parts and the water system always being contaminated no matter how many times they changed out the filtration systems. Quickly, however, it started turning into a nightmare for all on the island."

My ears perk up listening to James' tale. He has a way of drawing anyone in with how easily he can sell his stories on history.

"The first death happened as the workers were getting Santa's Sleigh Ride together. It's the only rollercoaster here on the island, but it circles the entire park with complicated loops and impossible twists. One worker was doing a safety check on the coaster's seat belt system when the ride started up on its own. The worker wasn't properly strapped in and was flung from the ride on the first drop. The people here started calling this place cursed after that incident because nothing was found on how the ride started by itself."

Well, that's going on the never-going-to-happen bucket list. I may be nuts, but riding a possessed coaster isn't something I feel I'd ever try. Unless you count my moment with Connor at Belgrove. He was sort of possessed at the time. I quickly dart a glance over at him to see him playing with a set of ornaments that jingle. If he wanted a jingling pair of balls in his hands, I have some just as good as those. Fuck, I really need to stop thinking about him. He doesn't want me the way I want him anymore. Just as the thought passes, I look over to see Jane now butting her head against his leg. Fucking traitor.

"The owners of the park were not so easily deterred. Setup went ahead no matter how many red flags took place that should have had this park shut down and production stopped. Opening day, visitors from all over came to the island. The ride operators weren't even properly trained on the equipment they were running, but the owners went ahead with the ribbon cutting ceremony and welcomed guests with bright smiles and excitement."

I know where this is headed. Death, gore, and massacre.

Otherwise, we wouldn't even be here right now.

"The first ride that set off the chain of tragedies was the swings. The crank broke, causing the swings to accelerate to speeds the machine should have never been programmed with. Once the chains started snapping and people started flying out, the pieces of the destruction started raining around to the other side of the park. The coaster lost part of its track when the chains of the swings slammed into it. The people on the coaster were thrown from their course and smashed right into the spinner ride. The spinner ride, in turn, popped the steel line holding up various lighting around the park and proceeded to sever people in half."

He really doesn't leave anything to the imagination. A shiver works its way up my spine from hearing all the haunting details surrounding this place until I have to tune him out. I look back at Connor again and find him smiling like a fucking lunatic at James' recount. Almost like he's being told his favorite bedtime story. He pats Jane's head but keeps his attention on James.

Turning away from him, I walk over to Mary, who has goose bumps raised all over her arms, and quickly bring her in for a hug. When she wraps her arms around me in return, I feel myself settle once more and kiss the top of her head. This girl is quickly becoming my center. I can honestly breathe easier when she's wrapped around me.

"Something's not right with Connor," she whispers so quietly that it only reaches my ears.

"I know, love. I know," I gently reply, looking at Connor once more to see him watching us with a sinister grin in place.

TWO

Conroy

There are so many tortured spirits here. It really is Christmas! I can see them everywhere lingering around, but they won't come near me even if their curiosity demands it of them. I'm the darkest entity on this island and even the dead recognize that. I shoo the mutt away with a wave of my hand as I lock my gaze on my two favorite people I love to fuck with.

"Would you stop looking at Nick and Mary like a fucking psychopath? You've already made Nick question my feelings for him. Stop doing the creepy shit or I'll find a way to banish you, bastard!" My ride-along growls at me from his passenger seat in this body.

"Aw. I remember a time when you were terrified of me. Did you find your balls, little boy? Or has that pussy made you courageous?" I coo back to him in my thoughts. His tiny little growl of anger in my head sounds out and I release a small chuckle, causing James to pause in his delightful tale of this place's destruction.

"You good, man?" he asks me with a look of concern.

"Never better," I reply with a thumbs up and a smile. James looks me up and down from head to toe before returning his attention back to the camera he's speaking into.

It's becoming harder and harder to have complete control over this flesh bag. Somehow, he keeps finding a way to shove me back and take over. Of course, the prick runs right into Nick's arms like a long-lost lover. I don't allow the shit for long, though. I'm not into guys. Mary's sweet pussy is plenty for me, for now. I love it when we play with her. Best part is she never knows the difference. I've gotten too good at mimicking Connor.

James continues with his history lesson as I turn and start looking through the remains of a place long forgotten. I can't help but notice a spirit lingering in the corner looking on at these oblivious fuckers like he'd give anything to take their place. I lock eyes with him and blow him a kiss. He looks downright petrified before he vanishes from sight. I shake my head at the scared little bitch and start creeping around the shop to get closer to Mary.

Jane growls and I instantly turn, registering a dark mist that forms where the spirit just was. I study it for a moment before I notice a grin on its form. I know damn well there isn't a damned soul here trying to challenge me. The shadow gives me a mock wave as I narrow my eyes, just like I did with the other spirit. Looking back at the others, I see they are completely unaware of our visitors.

"Well. How about that for a turn of events? How's it feel to be knocked down a peg, you dumbass?" Connor jeers at me. I forget sometimes he's able to see the spirit plane because of me.

"I'm starting to think you don't really like me, which is quite impossible. You may have freed me, but I freed you as well in return. Not so scared anymore, are you?" I quip back, feeling his rage. He really has come a long way since Belgrove. I should feel like a proud papa raising his boy up right, not that I would have any idea of the concept.

I hear a groan sound overhead and barely have enough time to grab Nick, Jane, and Mary before part of the roof fucking collapses right where they were standing. Mary is trembling, looking at the spot now covered with debris, and Nick looks like a gaping fish out of water, stunned at what just happened and his close call with death. Jane yips nervously, which starts to grate on my nerves, making me hiss a quick, "Quiet!" at her.

"Mary! Nick! Connor!" James shouts in panic.

"We're okay," I speak without thinking. That most likely was Connor taking over the reins from me for a moment. I feel his smug-ass smile and grit my teeth to maintain control.

"Th–thank you, Connor. That could have been terrible," Mary says to me, still shivering before turning and hugging me tightly. It feels really odd being shown genuine affection like this, and I awkwardly pat her back. I can fuck her into a coma, but cuddling isn't really in my playbook.

"Yeah, thanks, man. That could have fucking killed us," Nick comments when he finally finds his breath again. When he looks at me, I feel the longing in Connor to comfort him. Fuck that shit though. Out of all the humans I could have possessed, I got the one that does both.

"Fuck you! You just had no one to love you before, you jealous dick!" Connor snarls at me.

"No, Connor. I never needed love when I can just take whatever I want." I follow up my statement with a nice grab of Mary's ass. I'm instantly shoved away before Nick gets in my face.

"What the fuck is your problem, man!" he yells with spit flying from his mouth, bits of it landing on my face. It takes everything in me to channel the pussy whose body I'm coveting.

"Just getting in a hero grope. Stop being so hard up," I tease before giving him an easy smile.

"Everybody, chill. We're moving over to the workers' cabins to set up headquarters. Knock off the dumb shit so we can do our jobs and get paid," James orders, finally making his way over to us, grabbing Mary instantly and checking her over for injuries. Nick backs off, but his anger is clear. Connor radiates heartbreak while I soak it up like my favorite drink.

These fucks are so much fun to play with.

James

Tension is at an all-time high and it's not only because of what we endured at the haunted looney bin. Connor is acting strangely, almost bipolar in the way he flips through his moods. I'm not judging him because he experienced something altogether different from the rest of us.

Except for Mary.

My heart aches every time I think about her ordeal, not only through childhood, but then again in that fucking madhouse, and each time it enters my head, I make myself promise to protect her at all costs.

At all fucking costs.

We step out of the dilapidated Santa's Workshop and into a misting rain. The feel of it coating my skin causes goose bumps to rise to the surface. It's chilling when the wind hits the moisture and a shiver skates along my spine. We've been doing this for a while, scouting out supposedly haunted places and surviving its confines, but lately, I'm truly feeling like I need to call Sam and Dean for some serious exorcisms. Jane runs ahead, likely trying to find shelter against the storm moving in.

My eyes immediately flick to Connor with the thought, and I swallow down my suspicions again. He needs my support, not my accusation. Even though he's not always acting like the boy I grew up with doesn't mean he deserves to be constantly judged for it. I can see he's doing his best to move on from what we experienced at Belgrove.

"We have two choices. We can walk through the park to the cabins, or we can take that path." I point to a stone pathway completely overgrown with mangrove and cypress trees. "You guys choose."

Mary curls into my side, her hand resting over my chest as my heart begins to pound against her palm. There's no way she can't feel how she affects me. If she were any other girl, I'd hate them knowing my feelings, but when it's Mary, I want to express myself every chance I get. She's mine.

She's also Nick's and Connor's and I'm okay with that. Not only is she constantly protected, but we remain a tight-knit group, never having to worry about outsiders. I've been watching her slowly bond with Nick beyond friendship, and their relationship is so very different from ours. I can see how affected my brother is by Connor's ever-fluctuating moods, and Mary seems to be his grounding point, the person who pulls him out of his melancholy.

"We're going through the park," Connor insists. "That's why we're here, no? Start rolling the camera and let's pull up our big girl panties." See what I mean? He's never been like this before, but he does have a point. We did come here for the theme park. I wait for Mary and Nick to agree with the slight bob of their heads, and then we move forward. In front of us stands a large, crumbling train tipped on its side, and to the right of it stands a large post with a hook. Most likely it held a sign back in the day, but now a disintegrating Santa hat hangs from it. "Start up that mobile camera of yours," Connor snaps at me. "We want our patrons to see the horror that awaits."

"Cell phone, Connor," Nick says with exasperation. "This new speech of yours is fucking weird."

"Yes, yes," Connor waves him off with a roll of his eyes. "Cell phone camera."

An icy chill brushes by us, sending the rain to pummel against our skin a little harder, making us all huddle together a little closer, save for Connor, who's already approaching the train on his own.

"Maybe he feels like he has something to prove after what happened in Belgrove," Mary suggests, her cold arms circling my waist. As always, her touch sends sensations up my spine, making me shiver against her.

"Maybe he needs a good smack upside the head," Nick growls through his frustration. His eyes are narrowed on Connor's back and his mouth is set in an angry frown.

I give them the finger-to-mouth signal as I start up the live stream, the camera panning out to show Connor standing in front of that Santa hat while he stares at it eerily. His hands are sitting on his hips, his back curved slightly in a relaxed posture as a smirk coats his mouth.

"Hey, Phantom Hood! We're now entering the theme park section of this resort, the site of the carnage if you will. Many of the victims' families have stated they only received partial body parts of their loved ones while others received nothing. Some even tried to take the builders to court, only to be further disappointed when there was nothing they could be compensated with. It was hard to pin down who the investors were because no proper paperwork was ever filed, which put the state of Florida in hot water."

Connor jumps up at that precise moment and grabs the Santa hat, then walks over to us, looking triumphant as he puts it on his head. "Do you think this belonged to someone who was beheaded?"

Mary gasps and releases me from her arms just as Nick groans, but our PayPal begins to chime with his question, as insensitive as it is.

"The ribbon cutting happened right here in front of the train," I quickly say as I step around Connor and stride toward the crumbling train statue. "The staff and crew stood here with smiles etched on their faces, not knowing the horror that awaited them just a day later." I flip the camera around so I can look into the screen, hoping everyone can see the fear I'm not bothering to hide. "Beyond this point, there's no telling what we'll find. There have never been photos taken. No press dared step onto this island or fly overhead. There were rumors of the military posted on the island to prevent it, and the rumors of haunted curses were enough to keep this place undisturbed. It was all very mysterious and private. This will be the first time anyone has seen Silent Night Theme Park since 1976. If the military was ever here, they are no longer deeming this place a threat since we didn't see anyone on our way here."

Movement behind me on the screen catches my attention and I see fucking Connor adjusting the Santa hat onto his head, his boisterous chuckle reaching me. I swallow down my groan and stare into the camera.

"If you guys want to come on this *ride* with us, you know what to do." I quickly shut down the live stream and turn toward the other three, fury vibrating through my body. "What the fuck is wrong with you?" My voice raises a few octaves as I approach Connor, my hand clenching around my phone.

"Stop being a Debbie Downer," Connor moans. "I don't want a repeat of Belgrove. Can't we have fun with this one?"

The hat looks ready to fall apart on his head, the colors all faded and something looking like dried blood is dotted along the material. I open my mouth to berate him some more when all of our phones begin to ping with notifications; the chime telling us it's more PayPal deposits.

"Seems like we're doing something right," Nick murmurs as Connor wraps his arm around his neck to bring him in for an awkward hug.

"You got that right, buddy," Connor tells him, and I watch as my brother's face falls.

"I have never been your *buddy*," Nick sneers and shoves his arm away. "And you know it. I'm going to the boat to grab our bags."

"I'll come help!" I call out to Nick as I shoulder by Connor, giving him a nasty glare. "Are you going to be okay here?" I ask Mary, who's looking between us all with a worried look in her eyes and her adorable, pert nose crinkled.

"Of course." She nods.

I hurry after Nick, his long legs eating up the ground with each stride as if he has beef with the very earth beneath his feet. I empathize with his frustration because if that was me dealing with Connor's flippant attitude, I would've given up already.

"Nicky!" I call out, his name bouncing off his bulging back without acknowledgement.

I decide to let him have his moment, and when he's ready, I'll be here to help him in any way I can. I'm hoping Connor shakes himself free of whatever is holding him hostage and finally sees exactly how much my brother is worth.

With a quick look over my shoulder, I find Mary standing in front of Connor. Her head is tipped back, her hair kissing the bottom of her back, as she stares up into his face, a small smile playing around her mouth. Connor's hands are flying around animatedly, and he still has that disgusting hat on his head. He obviously feels absolutely nothing about the treatment he dishes out to my brother.

Watching them standing so close sends a chill through me, and not for the first time, I wonder if Mary is safe alone with him. I shake it off and curse myself internally, this isn't Belgrove and he's no longer Conroy.

Mary

Connor is in another one of his upswing moods as he excitedly speaks about walking through the theme park. I'm glad he looks so happy. I'm just not sure how long it will last.

"How about we just walk inside a little? Just to take a quick peek." His eyes widen as he gives me an innocent look.

"Only if you take that disgusting hat off your head." I chuckle. "I think it's covered in blood."

"I think it's awesome," he gushes as he pulls it off his head and slips it into his back pocket. "Let's go." He holds out his arm, waiting for me to link mine through as I chance a glance toward the boat, seeing James just stepping onto the dock. "They know you're safe with me."

I am safe with Connor. I think… Even now, I have a hard time separating Conroy at Belgrove from Connor at home.

No, I am safe with Connor. Especially if he stays in this mood.

"Fine, but just a peek," I warn him as I slip my arm through his, the touch of our skin causing an electric current to skate along my arm.

"James drew us a map," Connor says as he takes a folded piece of paper out of his front jeans pocket. "I wonder what we'll see first."

I clutch his elbow as he unfolds the paper, and I continue to stare ahead of us. Grass and moss are growing over the white cobblestone walkway, and the candy canes lining the lane are cracked and faded. Overgrown cypress trees are hanging low over the narrow walkway, giving the place an ominous look. I swallow down my trepidation as we walk under the low-swinging vines.

"First up is the Reindeer-Go-Round ride, the single attraction outside of the park meant for smaller children." The excitement in his voice is giving me the creeps. There's nothing about this place that feels like a family getaway. It's dark, smells odd, and it's cold here, despite what the forecast says it should be.

The trees sway with the breeze, revealing a large Merry-Go-Round with reindeer and Santa sleighs. I stop and yank on Connor's arm, holding him back. "We should wait for Nick and James."

"I just want some alone time with you, Mary," he whispers, making my head jerk upward to look at him with surprise. He's looking at me with desire, his eyes stripping me naked as they slowly roam over me. "It's been over a week since I've kissed you and your taste is all I can think about."

My heart jerks with an internal battle. I want him, I always have, but I know Nick does too, and it doesn't feel right making out with Connor when he's practically ignoring Nick.

"Connor…" I drag out the last syllable of his name in protest as I let go of him and wrap my arms around my waist. "It's not fair to Nick."

He steps into me, his arms encircling my waist, trapping my own in place, and bends down to press his mouth to my ear. "I could make you." And there it is, the warming between my thighs, the accelerated heartbeat. "I could force you onto the ride, place you inside one of those sleighs, and fuck you until you're crying for me to stop." A whimper escapes me as Connor becomes the version of himself I can't seem to resist. It's the depravity that lives inside of me, the need to be degraded and abused, and he knows it. "Follow me, baby girl. Right behind this tree and if they come, they won't see us."

I let him drag me behind the thick cypress tree and then I let him sink his fingers into my hair and give it a hard yank. My mouth meets his in a flurry of teeth and moans, our tongues swiping together in a frantic rush of need. Heat gathers between my legs, spreading into my lower stomach as lust tightens a coil I know all too well.

Logical thought escapes me as his hand slips up my shirt to grasp my breast in his hand, his long fingers squeezing to the point of pain. The ache only makes me curve my spine, drawing our bodies closer, and he chuckles as he pulls away to look into my eyes.

"How wet are you?" His rasp makes my clit pulse with need. "Tell me how wet you are here in the theme park graveyard. Tell the ghosts how badly you want me to suck your pussy."

"Holy fuck," I moan as my head hits the tree trunk. "I want that so much."

"Yeah, you fucking do." He drops to his knees as I gasp, watching him grip the waistband of my pants in his hands. "I better find you dripping, baby girl, or else my pretty pussy will be punished." I almost wish I wasn't fucking dripping wet. Punishment sounds more appealing. He drags my pants down to my ankles, taking my panties with them, and then his nose is pressed between my thighs as he takes an audible breath. "Fuck, baby, you want me this bad?" He forces my thighs apart and spreads my pussy open roughly, the sharp pain wringing another moan from my lips. "I want to fuck you so hard right now," he growls as his fingers continue spreading me. "I want to pound into your tight pussy."

"Connor, yes, please."

His fingers suddenly leave my most intimate place, the movement so quick I want to cry out for him to come back.

"Connor," he mocks me with a roll of his eyes. The attitude has my core clenching, wishing he would fill me up to the brim. He stands, leaving me with my back to the tree and my pants around my ankles as he crowds in close, his hand sealing around my throat. "One of these days, I'll have you screaming *my* name." His grip tightens as his tongue snakes along the shell of my ear, his breath hitting my neck like a humid summer breeze. He reaches around me with his other hand to roughly grab my ass in his palm, nearly pushing me over the edge. I'm so choked up with need that a keen leaves my lips right before he backs away with a knowing smirk on his lips. "You'll be begging for *me* before the night is out," he promises, just as James shouts my name, the sound echoing around our heads. "Better get dressed before your boyfriend and his brother find you wet for me."

I want to say they wouldn't care, but I'm not too sure about that. It does look like we snuck off to have alone time, and it makes me feel like a snake. We promised not to hide anything from each other, but this is feeling like something I need to keep to myself. For now anyway. Just until Connor and Nick figure their shit out.

Just as I pull my pants up and straighten my top, I hear the heavy footfalls of Nick and James' boots. Connor steps out into the lane with a shit-eating grin on his face, his arms crossed over his chest.

"Why didn't you wait for us?" James snaps.

"We didn't go far." Connor shakes his head. "Besides, Mary wanted to see the Reindeer-Go-Round." I let him blame me. It helps calm the guilt bubbling inside of me. I deserve it.

James gives me a knowing once-over as I step out from behind the tree. I bet my hair is slightly tangled from Connor's fingers and my mouth is a little too swollen from his brutal kiss. I can't hide my feelings for any of them, so all I can hope for is understanding.

"Is it in good shape?" Nick asks as he hoists a bag over his shoulder. He's avoiding meeting my eye, and it makes my stomach twist with anxiety.

"We didn't get that far," Connor says suggestively as he rocks back on his heels, his eyes looking smug.

"I bet," Nick grumbles as he drops all the bags in his hands to walk toward the ride, raking his fingers through his hair. Connor follows behind him as I turn to watch them walk away.

"That greedy pussy just wants what she wants when she wants it, huh?" James' words coat the side of my face in a warm rush of sin. "Is she still wet?" Before I can answer, James' hand comes around the front of me, thrusting into my pants in one smooth motion. His fingers run through my folds, gathering the damning moisture, and dragging it along my clit. His tut hits my ear with a chuckle at the evidence of my unsatisfied pussy. "Later, I'm going to have to spank her until she gushes."

Then, without another word, he pulls out of my pants and steps around me, slipping two fingers into his mouth. He sucks them loudly as he heads toward the ride, humming around the digits.

"I'm never going to survive them," I mumble as I trail behind him.

THREE

Nick

My stomach curdles as I let the image of Connor and Mary stepping out from behind that tree play on repeat in my mind. Her tangled curls looked as though hands were gripping into her scalp, her lips swollen and red, and her chest heaving with lust. I was fucking jealous, and it had nothing to do with the fact that they were together, but that he was showing her the attention I long for.

"You're acting like a little girl again," he sneers from close behind me, making my fists curl and my knuckles crack with anger.

"Shut up," I snap as I approach the Reindeer-Go-Round.

This area of the park was left untouched by the devastation, but it didn't survive the test of time. Weeds and moss have reclaimed the land the ride sits on, their green growth slowly climbing along its surface. The reindeer have eerie, enormous smiles on their faces, and the sleighs all have a Santa sitting inside, his face looking more like something out of a horror movie than the North Pole.

"Fuck," Connor curses, his voice filled with glee. "This place was for children? It feels like a horror theme park based in the North Pole." His thoughts closely match my own.

I step up onto the base as James and Mary round the corner, Mary's face a mask of guilt. I can't stand to look at either of them or their pity, so I sit in the first sleigh that doesn't have a front-row seat to their approach. The inside of the sleigh is covered in green muck and moss, but I don't care about any of that as my ass hits the hard seat.

I just need space to think.

My alone time is quickly disrupted as the space beside me is suddenly engulfed with the scent of musk and sin. His heat scorches along my arm and leg, making me huff with annoyance but also long for him with desire. I want his mouth to make my lips swell with the brutality of his kisses. I want his fingers to tousle my hair in a fit of lust-filled need.

"Nick." He sounds winded and tired as he grabs my hand, making my head shoot up to look him in the eyes. "Don't... give up... on me. I'm just not myself."

The sound of his voice and the vulnerability in his words are so familiar to me, as if the boy I've loved for so long has resurfaced through his layers of moods. It rips the frustration out of me and is quickly replaced with a fervor to be with him, like I don't have much time.

I reach for him at the same time his hands grip my shirt to pull me closer. Our mouths clash in a desperate attempt to hold on to each other, to keep these versions of ourselves here. The sounds of Mary and James approaching do nothing to quell the desire, and I give in to the tidal wave, submerging myself in what I know will kill me in the end.

But I can't stop it.

"Mary, let's take a walk," I hear James coax as my tongue snakes along Connor's. Is it weird that I think I can taste her in his mouth? And weirder still that I could come in my pants from the flavor of them intertwined?

I work at the button and zipper on his jeans, his hips lifting to help me haul them down to pool around his ankles. His boxers are tented with the evidence of his hunger, and my mouth waters at the sight. I want him in my mouth and coming down my throat; the need is so fucking strong.

My knees hit the unforgiving floor of the sleigh as I pull his hard cock out of his underwear. His groan rises from his chest in a loud rumble and escapes his mouth, the sound making my own cock pulse with need.

I lean forward and suck him into my mouth, loosening my jaw to accommodate his girth. His taste floods my tongue, drawing a moan from me and making my balls tighten in anticipation. I haven't had a proper release since Belgrove. It's as if my body needs him to accept us for what we are before it absorbs any pleasure.

Connor's hips lift once more, pushing his cock farther down my throat, and then he sighs as I gag around him, his throat cording tight as his head falls back against the sleigh. I want him to look at me, to watch me devour him, but I don't have the strength to argue. I'll take whatever scraps of affection he tosses my way, swallowing them whole and begging for more.

His hand slips through my hair as he forces me to suck him to a rhythm only he can direct, and again, I let him do it, giving him full rein of my body. He fucks my throat at a bruising pace, the grip on my hair tightening to the point of pain, each follicle ripping out into his palm.

Each thrust is punctuated by a grunt as he nears his end, the sounds heightening the lust gathering around our small sanctuary of hedonistic pleasure. He pounds into my esophagus, each impact of his cock sending the most pleasurable pain straight to mine. My body is begging for release, but I refuse to acknowledge it until Connor is finished and sated.

With a muffled groan, his warm cum slips down my throat, the thick fluid coating my tongue as it shoots from his tip. I swallow every drop, eager to taste him and feel his warmth inside of me. I release his cock as it begins to soften, having sucked it completely clean, and look up at him with a smile. Only, I find him scowling back.

Connor quickly stuffs himself back into his pants as he mumbles and curses under his breath. His eyes are focused on his hands as if he refuses to acknowledge me here on my knees in front of him. It's like a sharp slap to the face, one I've been taking several times a week since we left Belgrove.

As I'm about to rise, his hand lands on my head, and I look up at him as hope swells inside of me once again.

"Thanks, man," he says as he pats the top of my head. "That was talent. Let's catch up with the others."

He stands, leaving me there on my knees, my body stiff with shock. One more pat on the head and he leaves the sleigh, whistling the tune of "Winter Wonderland." The sound of his jovial song shatters my already broken heart into a million shards, and I vow to never let him get the better of me again.

I love Connor, but this man he's becoming is not the same one my heart has been longing for and I can feel myself slowly detaching from him. It's painful, torturous even, but I refuse to give him my fragile heart, only to watch him stomp it to bits at my feet.

Conroy

"I have to admit, your boyfriend sucks dick like a fucking champ," I tell the boy who's sulking inside of me, and laugh when he huffs in annoyance.

I can feel the way his heart is breaking; how heavy it sits in my new, cavernous chest. Poor thing, is this what tragic first love feels like? Love wasn't something I became acquainted with when I was alive. I only knew depraved sin and lust. Cravings and longings.

Never did I hand the black organ, pumping immoral blood through my veins, to anyone. Not even Mommy dearest. She owned my cock, but never my heart.

My thoughts are quickly interrupted when I stumble upon Mary and James, both of them holding each other's hands and staring into the theme park. Do they always have to touch?

This is usually when the young boy inside of me snaps back with a retort, telling me I'm evil and the such, but he's awfully quiet right now, his heart growing heavier by the second. Maybe some alone time with the girl would put him back on the right track.

Someone knocks into my shoulder, making me stagger to the side a few steps, and when I look up, I watch Nick stride by. The way his jaw is set, and the vein pulsing at his temple tells me he's upset too. Well, good. Two men don't make a right. He'll be happy I broke up this charade before he really got too attached.

He stands beside Mary, who also takes his hand, and I roll my eyes at the wholesome threesome in front of me. The world now is so very different from what I remember. One girl didn't have two boyfriends—*"Three,"* the defeated voice inside my head corrects.

Right, I nod as a smile creeps over my mouth; she has me too.

"Let's get to the cabin so we can get set up," Mary says softly to

James and Nick. I notice her giving Nick's hand a slight squeeze and my head tilts, wondering what emotion she's giving him right now.

"It's called pity and sympathy, you fucking asshole," my cling-on answers my thoughts. *"And I'm not the damn cling-on, dickhead. You are."*

Trailing behind the others, I process Connor's words. Sympathy is foreign to me. A doctor once told me that in order to be able to feel an emotion, it must first be given to you. I've never been given sympathy before, therefore I have none.

"So you all use being a little bitch as your tactic to get pussy instead of just taking it like sweet Mary desperately wants," I deduce and get answered back with a scoff. I chuckle slightly and continue skipping along with the others in the lead.

A small whimper has me freezing in my tracks and looking around the desolate wonderland of horrors. The others are oblivious to it and continue on their way, never once looking back at me. I'll process that later. I should be the center of those motherfuckers' universe, after all.

The tiny cry comes again as I sneak around a huge present statue, the paint cracked and peeled from its surface. That black mist is back from Santa's workshop and seems to be tormenting a child's soul. Rage fills me to the brim before I can bury the feelings. These assholes can't know. I swore to keep the shit buried alongside my rotting corpse.

"What the hell was that?" Connor asks in shock.

"Nothing you need to concern yourself with. That fucker has a meal I want myself."

"You're fucking sick!" Connor screams and I smile despite the torrent of not feeling an ounce of remorse.

I approach the mist, feeling the darkness rising within me. The small soul withdraws further into itself, trying so hard to disappear. It's my burden to carry. It's my curse.

"Hey, fucker. That kid's mine now. His soul belongs to me," I coo over at the kid. The cries intensify as the mist seems delighted to have another tormentor in its area.

"You're damned too?" the slithering voice questions me. It

feels like knives being dragged across my skin as lemon juice is pouring right behind the blade. A trickle drips from my ears and I reach up to see a smear of blood on my fingers. This kind of evil taints a place so much that nothing but tragedy will be seen. No wonder this park failed so miserably.

"Nah. You see, I'm a bit different. I own this whole place now. The souls, the spirits, the fucking stagnate air you float in. It's mine," I answer, feeling Connor trying to shrink away from the blackness starting to crave my insides. This bastard mist tried challenging me. You don't challenge a king.

"We'll see about that," it hisses back before vanishing. The child looks like it up and died again from the sinister energy still lingering.

"Run along, kid. I'm really bored now." I shoo at it with my hands and the child's eyes widen slightly before vanishing as well.

I feel Connor perk up in my head as his thoughts start tumbling into mine.

"Well, holy shit. You, Conroy Davies, are a fucking liar." My only response is to snarl as he pieces together a puzzle that was never meant to be solved.

Silent Night Theme Park

FOUR
Mary

"To get to the cabins from where we're standing, we have to continue through the park, unless we backtrack and take that overgrown path," James reads from the map in his hands. His brows are crumpled in thought as his tongue snakes out along his bottom lip.

I don't know what's wrong with me lately, but Belgrove unlocked something inside of me, and now I see each one of my best friends as a quick ride to an orgasm.

Or are they my boyfriends?

"I see the way you're staring at him. Have I left you feeling a bit needy, Mary?" Connor's deep voice skims over my ear, the heat of his breath warming my cheek as his body drifts closer to my back.

My brain shuts down all thought as Nick crowds into his brother, both of them standing in front of me and staring down into the map as my ass presses backward into Connor's extremely hard cock. His low groan of pleasure washes over me, causing my nipples to harden into painful peaks and press against my tank top.

Even so, I need a little more.

That depraved voice in my head tells me that I'm nothing more than a slut needing three men, and even though I can feel my own humiliation, perpetrated by my own thoughts, I need someone else to agree.

I need someone else to make me feel dirty.

A fresh coating of shame slips over me, ripping a soft moan from my slightly parted lips, making Connor chuckle behind me.

"You are quite the little slut, aren't you, my pretty, little girl?"

Something tickles the back of my mind, a memory I've buried away with the others that I never want to think of again, but the feeling is familiar. Fear and self-loathing. It feels like I'm transported back there. The pitch-black, the cot, and the inability to stop what's happening. I'm back inside Belgrove as my pussy clenches and my skin breaks out in a sheen of moisture.

Maybe it's the sound of Connor's voice and his chosen words at this moment, the coincidence too close to what I endured inside those haunted walls.

His tongue slips along my ear as a shiver wracks my body. His hands encircle my waist, and I lean my head back against his chest, wanting him with every cell in my body. The only thing that hauls me out of the moment is the thought of hurting Nick more. I don't want him to see Connor giving me the affection he's so desperately craving.

"We'll continue this later when everyone's asleep," he whispers and releases me to head toward the others.

I place a hand around my neck, letting the rapid flutter of my pulse beat against my fingers. My body is strung so tight, teetering on the edge of combustion, and just when I think it can't get any worse, James turns to look at me over his shoulder, casting me a devilish wink.

"Fuck," I exhale through my teeth.

"Looks like we're heading into the worst of it, Mary," Nick says as he gives Connor a wide berth and heads my way. "Stick with me, okay?"

"What's the worst of it? Do we have an idea before we head in?" My eyes are on James, because if there's anything to be found out, he already knows it.

"I would imagine years of weather exposure and nature have concealed a lot of what happened. There should be a lot of destruction telling a story of horror. I can't tell you anything else because there wasn't much I could find on it. The workers who got off the island were forced to sign an NDA, so everything I find are rumors," James informs me, his eyes soft and lined with fear. We all hate the unknown.

"Let's do this." Connor claps his hands and walks ahead.

Nick's hand slips into mine, giving me the strength to take the necessary steps toward the looming gates with a large, metal sign hanging from above it, leaving the entrance and entering the theme park. Silent Night is embossed on the surface of the rusted sheet.

James stops in front of us as we all stand there looking up at the precariously hanging metal and Connor chuckles darkly as he steps under. No sense of preservation to be found.

"This is the section with the rides," James mutters, uncertainty coating his words. His hand grips the paper map tightly, the crinkling sounds breaking up our heavy silence.

"We got this," I murmur and step under the gates, dragging Nick with me.

"Yeah," James agrees as he follows.

Connor has disappeared into the park, his eerie whistling sounding so very far away. Our boots clip off the cobblestone path with loud *thuds* as we slowly enter the grounds. The path is overgrown with moss and grass, the long blades skimming my waist, and the air begins to grow heavier the farther in we go, as if in an ominous warning.

I suck in a large breath as the massive, wooden track of a roller coaster appears in the distance. From here I can see large portions of it missing, as if gouged out by a giant's hand. The three of us stop and slowly take in our surroundings to the strange soundtrack of Connor's whistle.

First up is a large sleigh ride to our right, the same type of ride I've ridden at many carnivals; only the ones I went on were boats. The idea of it is to swing back and forth, slowly gaining momentum until each swing brings it perpendicular to the ground.

The red-painted fiberglass is faded and warped, and the sleigh is sitting on its side, having fallen off its structure. Or worse, judging by the severely cracked surface.

"Shit," James hisses and my head snaps up to look at him, following his eyesight to the left. "That's where it started. The swing ride."

A large, circular structure sits on the ground, the metal long rusted along with the heavy chains hanging from it. A little corrugated metal booth stands beside it, the surface coated with dark stains. I swallow down the horror that's creeping up inside of me as we look upon what can only be described as destruction.

And there, standing in the center of it all is Connor.

He's staring downward at something in front of the booth, his whistling reaching a higher pitch. His shoulders are relaxed, his hands tucked into the pockets of his pants, and his right foot tapping along with his tune.

"Since when did Connor whistle?" James asks.

"What the fuck is he looking at?" Nick grunts out.

I don't pull my eyes away from Connor, and he seems to sense it as he turns slightly, his eyes meeting mine with glee.

He tips back on his heels as his mouth stretches into a wide grin. "You guys should come see this."

To my surprise, it's me who starts forward, curiosity taking over the fear. My hand slips from Nick's and I move toward Connor, watching as he continues to grin at the shattered pieces of the ride. Just the sight of his elation has a chill running over my skin. He wasn't like this for any of our other haunted stays. He's always been the cautious one, our voice of reason.

"What is it?" I ask him as I stop a foot from his back. "What are you looking at?"

"I can see it all," he mumbles, his voice sounding awed as his hands swipe over the wreckage. "The screams, the blood…" His words are almost lust-filled as he takes a large breath in through his nose. "I can smell the fear."

"Connor," I say his name with caution. "Are you okay?"

I look over my shoulder to find Nick and James huddled together, both of them watching us with trepidation. They can sense this isn't normal either.

"His hands wrapped around this crank as he tried to pry it back," he says, his words dancing like a melody of cheerfulness. "When that didn't work, he yanked hard on it, only to watch in horror as the metal bar snapped in half. This ride quickly became the epicenter of mass slaughter."

"How could he know that?" James breathes out as he and Nick appear at my side. "There's no account of that."

I step around Connor and look down at the twisted metal rod protruding from a rusted metal box, sitting in front of the small booth with the windows shattered. The metal looks like it's stained with more than rust, and I swallow thickly at the sight. Blood, matter, flesh. Any of it could be a possibility.

"Look at this place…" Connor spreads his arms wide and does a quick spin. "It's a treasure trove of torture. I bet the staff cabins are teeming with spirits just waiting to tell us their horrible ends."

"You should be catching this on live," Nick whispers to James. "He's acting out of character, but the people would eat this up."

James

I quickly start up the live stream just as Connor steps up to the ride and leans forward to grab a rusted chain in his hands. The sounds of scraping metal and creaking iron fill the air, and when Connor turns to face the camera, he has a spine-chilling look on his face. His eyes are wide with excitement and the smile that curves along his lips looks so foreign.

"You guys are lucky. I can sense everything that happened, and I can't wait to tell you all about it," Connor says as he drops the chain and walks toward me, his eyes on the phone. "Maybe it's because I've felt what it was like to be on the other side. Regardless, you're all in for a treat."

He turns and heads for the small path leading to the center of the park, his whistling getting eaten up as the winds begin to gust harder. I turn off the phone and stare at Mary and Nick as more pings sound from our PayPal apps.

"There's something not right," Mary remarks, her voice being drowned out by the pings. "Could he be possessed again?"

"You guys better hurry," Connor calls out seconds before the rain pelts our skin. "There's a storm coming in."

A loud rumble of thunder rolls over our heads as I look into Nick's face and say, "He's never been here before. How could he…?"

"Let's go." Nick grabs Mary's hand and we all start running through the park, our sights blurred by the pounding rain, preventing us from seeing too much of the surrounding destruction.

We end up at a chain-link fence with signs every few feet indicating staff quarters and no patrons allowed beyond that point. The fence is bowed and partly collapsed, but it does open up to another path leading through dense trees.

Mary wraps her arms around her waist as her skin erupts with goose bumps from the rain. Her hair hangs down around her shoulders in wet ringlets and her mouth begins to quiver from the chill. Connor has long disappeared down the path, the cypress vines swaying from his disturbance and the wind. Nick lets go of Mary's hand and heads in next as I gather a scared and cold-looking Mary to my chest.

"I love you," I state over her head as she gasps. "I just wanted you to know that before we go any farther."

"I love you too." Her words are muffled against my chest, but I hear each syllable clearly.

I turn her around by her shoulders and keep her back close to my chest as I guide her onward. I won't let anything happen to her. She's the single, most important thing in my life.

Her body trembles again as we head down the path, more from apprehension than the chilly rain I would assume. Just as Nick and Connor's angry voices become clearer, the sunken roofs of cabins appear between the tree trunks. My grip on Mary's shoulders tightens as the argument ahead of us grows louder.

"How could you know that?" Nick exclaims. "The door plates are rusted through. There are no names anymore."

"Just trust me, kid," Connor sneers, setting off a growl to erupt from Nick's throat.

"Kid?!" Nick hollers just as we clear the treeline and find a row of ramshackle cabins.

"No, Nick!" Mary screams just as my brother tackles Connor to the ground, both of them landing with loud grunts.

She shrugs my hands off her shoulders and darts forward as I groan at the sight in front of me. It's been a long time coming, and I knew my brother was on the edge of an explosion. I'm actually surprised he lasted this long.

"Mary!" I call at her back, making her turn to look at me with desperation. "Don't get between them. You could get hurt."

I stride for her and tuck her behind me as I approach the brawlers tumbling across the tall grass.

"They're going to hurt each other," Mary cries. "Make them stop, James."

I grab her hand and pull her to my side, cradling her head under my chin. "I think we should leave them to it. They need to work out some of that aggression. Connor can't keep disrespecting my brother because he's confused. Let's check out this cabin they were standing in front of."

She whimpers but follows me with little resistance as I move toward the cabin with a rusted plate screwed into the warped, wood surface of the door. It would be nice to get out of the rain, but heading into another confined space and this time on a haunted island is enough to give me hesitation and pneumonia.

With Mary's well-being in mind and wanting to get her out of the cold rain, I bury my fears down deep and push the door the rest of the way open.

The creaking noise is like nails on a chalkboard as the door slowly opens and reveals the inside of the cramped space. Before I've even registered what I'm looking at, Mary lets loose a hair-raising scream, startling Nick and Connor from their Royal Rumble in the rain.

Nick

Mary's scream snaps me out of the violence flowing freely through my veins as I land one last punch into Connor's stupidly solid abs. His laughter sickens me as I feel the dark torment of his treatment tumble around my mind. My confusion has paved the way to anger and I can't hold it at bay anymore, but the thought of Mary in trouble puts my moral compass back in the right place for a moment.

We both scramble up from the ground and take off running for the cabin. The first thing I see when I slam through the door is Mary shaking so hard in James' arms and my brother's terror. My big brother is never fucking scared. Connor shoves in beside me, snarling like a caged animal, and starts pacing the cabin.

Fuck it.

I pace along with him, ready to rip shit apart and figure out what did this to the ones I love. Just as Connor goes to shatter a lamp in the corner, James' arm snaps out and grabs his wrist as the smallest scratching sound reaches our ears.

"I don't sense anything. There's fucking nothing here that could fuck with my girl," Connor whispers so quietly, lost in thought, but I'm close enough to hear it. My heart fills and yet shatters again. He said 'My girl' not 'Our girl.'

I turn toward the scraping sound and slowly ease down to look under the bed it's coming from. Darkness floods my sight other than the smallest ray coming from the setting sun. The littlest shadow shoots from one corner of the bed to the other and my eyes track it.

I hear James behind me, trying to soothe Mary and calm her down.

"Mary, what happened?" I finally think to ask as my eyes stay focused on the entity drifting in circles. Before she can answer, the black mass seems to explode right in my face as another ear-shattering scream sounds out around us.

"NICK!" my brother bellows, but I'm too busy trying to get my hands in front of my face as a terrible screeching fills the cabin's space. I see Connor run over to me from the corner of my eye and lift his foot like he's about to stomp my skull in, and my brother yells a warning and tries to reach me at the same time.

At the last second, his foot comes down right beside my head and a violent crunch rings in my ears. Turning my face slightly, I see the rat that Connor has just ended, flattened under his shoe.

"Motherfucking, crazy-ass bastard," James says as he grabs Mary and hauls her outside.

Looking back up at Connor, I see him heaving for air and looking lost in a daze as he mumbles. "I got it. It didn't hurt you. I got there in time." My heart flips thinking maybe my near-death experience with the fucking rat finally got through to him and a small piece of hope starts beating as furiously as my heart is.

"Hey," I gently try to pull him from whatever episode is going on in his head. "It was just a rat. I'm okay." I watch his features slowly transform from lost and unsure to fucking evil in the blink of an eye and it hits me like a ton of bricks to the fucking face.

"Like I give a fuck if it ate your intestines. I was only trying to shut Mary up from her whimpering," he responds with a smirk, and that darkness slithers back into me.

I jackknife up and tackle him again, taking him down to the cabin floor, and start wailing into him as his hysterical laughter rings out.

Conroy

The pain from Nick's attack sends a thrill through my pores as Connor screams mercilessly at me for being a sick motherfucker. I can't even write off the growing piece of meat between my thighs as accidental because this is the most I've felt alive in a long, goddamn time.

"Keep going, make it hurt more," I egg him on. I sense the black tide in him and it brings out an excitement in me to corrupt someone to the edge of this kind of madness. Once Nick is spent and sweating from the physical fight leaving him, I smile wickedly behind bloody teeth as the thunder outside rocks the cabin we're in. "Did it feel good, boy? Did it make you feel alive?" I demand and lock eyes with him. He stares down at me, unsure of himself and the damage he's caused, before slamming his lips to mine. I shove as hard as I can to get him off me, but this asshole is built like a brick fucking wall. He picks his head up for a moment and smiles that same evil smile I normally carry. Unease prickles my spine at the monster I've unleashed.

"You won't give me Connor back, then I'll just have to take your advice and fuck you out of him. How about that, Conroy?" he snarls before taking my lips once more. I hear Connor's laughter and cheers ring out and have no fucking choice but to hand over the reins to rid myself of the lust Nick is giving off in heaps. Smart little fucker was the first one to figure it out once again.

I shove him off of me just enough to speak. "You can have thirty fucking minutes with your lover boy, then I get the bag of flesh back to fuck Mary with and forget this shit is about to happen. Agreed?"

"You don't get to make demands, you sick fuck. Give me Connor back right now or I'm going to have my cock so far up your ass you'll be begging me to stop."

This shithead isn't giving in. Touché, you fucking prick. Touché. It's my last thought as I let go and let the only home of darkness take me.

Connor

The change happens so suddenly that I have zero time to react as Nick presses me harder into the floor and desperately begs between kisses to have me back with him. He feels the moment I'm me again as I kiss him back with an urgency he's come so used to knowing.

"Why!?! Fucking why didn't you say something!" he screams before peppering kisses down my neck and nibbling my collarbone.

"I was fucking scared of what would happen! I didn't want to stay at Belgrove. I wanted to come home with you and Mary," I cry out as he roughly grabs my aching cock.

"You're going to learn never to hide shit from me ever again," he growls out before ripping at the button of my jeans. He strips me with a quickness that has me in a daze before tearing off his own belt and looping it into makeshift handcuffs. Strapping my hands together, he lifts my arms above my head before biting down hard on my neck. I yell out as the pain assaults me and I struggle to get away from it. My cock pulses and confuses the fuck out of me. I'm enjoying this kind of torture. Nick rolls me over, keeping me pinned to the floor still. "I want you to keep your fucking hands above your head and lift your ass up in the air. The moment you move your hands, I will fucking stop. Are we clear?" he breathes into my ear so fucking sensually that my brain wants to melt.

"Yes, sir," I sass and go to lift my ass up. A sharp pain explodes on my ass cheek as I yelp and almost move my hands to rub at the aching sting left behind. Only his words bring me to hold steady because while I want the pleasure I know he will bring me, I also know I deserve this punishment for hiding Conroy from him.

"You had me out of my mind worried you didn't fucking love me anymore," he says and my heart somersaults in my chest. Before I can even respond, another smack lands on the opposite cheek and I clench my teeth together from the sting. "You drove me insane and made me question myself," he speaks again before another smack lands on the same spot in rotation. Five more smacks are delivered in rapid succession before I cry out at the fire starting to eat me alive. I'm just about to lift my hands when a hot, wet tongue lands right on my fucking hole and I jolt as the pleasure it causes shoots directly into my balls.

"Fuck, Nick," I groan as he laps at me and massages the sting out of my cheeks. I keep my face pinned to the floor and my hands high above my head while trying to breathe through the orgasm wanting to tear me apart. I feel his hand move from my cheek as pressure from his finger starts opening me up.

"Bear down on my finger, baby. Let me in this tight little ass," Nick tells me, and I do as he asks. Pushing out, he slides into me almost effortlessly. Maybe it's because of all the pain from my still throbbing ass or I've reached a level of fucked I can't explain, but I feel nothing other than complete ecstasy as he thrusts his digit in and out of me. He continues to drive me to the brink before backing off and adding another finger, stretching me and lapping at me all the while.

I'm ready to lose my load when he suddenly pulls out of me and I cry out at the loss. I start to speak to curse him out when a different pressure starts seeking entrance to my ass.

"Nick?" I question as I feel his cock pushing gently into me. I have no idea when he even got naked with me, so lost in the pleasure he was wringing out of me.

"Shh, baby. Just like with my fingers. Bear down on me. Let me in," he coos softly. I'm on edge, so I do exactly as he says again. I wish he'd let me see his face or let me kiss him as he takes my fucking ass virginity, but I guess this is part of the punishment and I have no regrets about being with him like this. Mary and I may have been together, but this is my first time full-on with another man. As the burn intensifies, I feel his head make it past my ring. He backs off as I feel cool liquid drip down my crack and it causes me to clench a bit. Now he's got me wondering if he just carries lube around in his pocket like an everyday item. Normal people have car keys, Nick, however, has lube. I chuckle at the thought which earns me another smack to the ass as he starts to sink deeper into me. Nick hisses out a sound of pleasure and it brings a smile to my face, knowing he is as lost in this moment as I am.

When he pushes back in again, I feel his piercing pop in this time and my eyes cross as it glides across my walls. Something like this should be illegal to feel as my cock throbs with the need to come.

He slowly thrusts until he's fully seated inside of me, only stopping to let me adjust to his girth as I grunt and try to get him to move.

"Calm down, baby. We're just getting started. I want to fucking savor you." His hands follow the path of my spine before running up my hips. I shiver at the easy touches and will myself to calm down. He leans over me and I feel the warmth of his chest meeting my back. His kisses on the back of my neck feel like a balm I need on my soul. "I waited for this for a long time. I'm going to fucking devour you, Connor. You aren't allowed to leave me again. Do you understand? You fucking fight him and come back to me." He follows his declaration with a quick thrust of his hips, and I yell out as the feel of his cock stretching me almost sends me into oblivion. Keeping his chest to my back, he reaches around and grabs hold of my length, jacking me in tune with his thrusts.

"Oh, fuck! Please! I won't ever keep shit from you again. OH, GOD! I'll always come back to you!" I beg and plead, wanting him to end this madness he's inflicted on me. I think I'd agree to any goddamn thing if he'd just stop trying to make my dick and my heart explode at the same time.

"He doesn't get to have control of you. This is your fucking body. Say it!" Nick orders, still thrusting into me and driving me out of my mind as his thumb plays with the head of my cock.

"He doesn't get to have control!" I all but squeal. I know how I want to die now. It's with Nick's fucking dick in my ass.

"That's my good boy. Come for me, baby," he demands, giving me the fucking permission I didn't realize I was waiting for. He lifts slightly, letting go of my cock to grab my hips, and starts to piston in and out of me. The sound of his hips slapping off my ass fills the room and I cry out when my cock starts dripping cum instead of ropey spurts.

"Oh fuck. What the hell is happening?" I cry out, feeling the tears running down my face as my cock continues to leak against Nick's hammering.

"That's called a male orgasm, baby. Not normal ejaculation. I want you ruined for anyone else." Nick chuckles before showing me mercy and gripping my length to help finish me off. He groans in my ear as I feel him grow slightly and pulse inside of me.

We both drop to the dank floor together as he takes my hands out of the bindings and massages them, bringing the feeling back to my fingertips. I roll over and he brings his lips to mine so tenderly that I start crying for a different reason.

"I love you, Nick. I never meant to leave you." Telling him how I finally feel is freeing, to say the least.

"I know that now, babe. We'll figure this out together. No more of this stupid bullshit," he says, kissing the top of my head. I lay my head over his chest and listen to the sound of his pounding heartbeat as I feel the evidence of his passion leaking out of me.

"Uh, so. Don't think there's a working shower anywhere on this cursed island, do you?" I crack out, drawing little hearts on his abs with my finger. His answering silent laughter brings me the first bit of peace since Belgrove.

FIVE

James

The rain soaks through our clothes as I guide Mary to the next cabin, leaving behind the sounds of Connor and Nick's fighting. They need to figure out their shit, and then we all need to get our heads back into the game. A sharp bark comes from Jane as she runs ahead, her fur looking worse from the rain.

When she stops at the next cabin door and sniffs under it, Mary stops and watches her as her body trembles next to mine.

"Wait to see if she can sense anything," she suggests.

"We need to get you out of the rain," I insist as I try to rub some warmth into her thin arms.

"Just wait, James," she huffs out just as Jane lifts her scraggly head and begins to pant, her tail wagging back and forth.

"Let's go." I pull Mary forward and give Jane a quick pat on the head as I push in the cabin door. "Good girl." I swear the fucking dog preens as much as Mary does when I say it to her.

We both step over the threshold, both wary of any wayward animals besides the fucking dog. Jane takes her time sniffing around the room and when we see and hear nothing, we physically relax.

"What is it about these places and the damn animals?" Mary mutters as we step inside the cramped space.

"There are no humans here to force them away from what was

first their home," I tell her.

"Oh," she breathes out. "That makes sense." Jane curls up beside the small, rickety table in the corner and lets out a loud exhale. As soon as my eyes have adjusted to the dark, I release Mary from my arms and begin to look through the stuff left in here. "It's as if the person ran off the island without ever taking their stuff," Mary says as she fingers an open suitcase on the floor, its contents hanging out over the edges.

"Or they never made it out of the theme park," I whisper.

"Right." She nods, her wet curls swaying with the motion. "Look, the suitcase has a tag on it." She pulls on the small, rectangular sleeve and it breaks away from the suitcase handle easily. "Daniel Harris," she reads off the tag. "From West Palm Beach."

"What else is in that suitcase?" I ask as I roam around the room, looking for anything that'll give us more clues about what happened on this island.

I find a few photographs sitting on top of the small dresser; the edges curled, and the paper yellowed from time. One is of a young girl, no more than ten years old with dark, curly hair, sort of reminding me of Mary at that age. The other is of an older girl in a bikini, her hip jutted out with a seductive smile on her lips. This one, I would assume, was Daniel's girlfriend.

"His passport is here," Mary says excitedly. "And, James, the paperwork for his employment is here."

"No fucking way!" I exclaim as I rush over to her.

We're trespassing on the island, hoping that with time, nothing is being monitored and we can find out exactly what transpired here. Mary has stumbled upon a gold mine, and we could potentially blow this whole thing wide open.

We both sit on the bed and Mary squeals when it shakes a little. The moisture in this room has slowly begun to rot the furniture, but we lucked out with Daniel's clothing still being in his suitcase because it protected the paperwork at the bottom.

"He was eighteen, freshly graduated from high school, and this was his first job," Mary begins as she reads through his paperwork.

I flip open his passport and find a young kid looking back at me with dark, curly hair, similar to the girl's in the photo, and some peach fuzz growth on his face. There are no stamps on his passport, showing he had never traveled before.

"Is there a company name?" I ask Mary.

"Concord Amusement Inc." The words are said into the small room, and we're both stunned into silence. Concord Amusement was one company accused of funding this place, and even though I did some thorough digging on both the internet and the dark net, I found nothing to back up that claim. "Aren't they…?"

"Fairytale Attractions now, yeah," I answer her.

"Oh my gosh, James, this contract has a list of other theme parks and resorts they own. Here it says, given how busy this theme park gets, people may be shuffled around accordingly."

"What's on the list?"

We both lean over the stack of papers in her hands and most of the theme parks we see have long closed, nothing standing out in our memories until we see the name of a resort on the last line. A place that's come up often on our blog site for us to visit. Another place riddled with a dark past.

"Lovers Cove Getaway," I whisper. "They owned Lovers Cove Getaway."

Jane chooses that moment to dart up from her sleep with a loud howl and runs out of the door. The sound startles Mary, who screams and tosses the papers up in the air, making them rain down around us as she jumps into my lap and wraps her body around me.

My cock hardens involuntarily as Mary's damp body and scent floods my senses. I can't help that I'm like a fucking teenager whenever she touches me, but maybe this time I can help her get over her fear of all things haunted.

As she's shivering and whimpering in my arms, I shove my hand through her wet hair and give the thick strands a yank, forcing her head backward. This time when she whimpers, it ends with a long, drawn-out moan.

"James," she groans. "Here?"

My lips hit her ear as I say, "Do whores like you get a choice?"

"No," she breathes out as she presses down against my cock.

"Tell me exactly what you are and I'll give you what you need." My other hand skims down her back to grab onto the thick globes of her ass as her arms tighten around my neck.

"I'm a dirty slut," she admits, the sentence ending in another low moan. I will never understand why she enjoys this or even needs it, but it's not for me to understand. I'm only here to make sure she feels safe and loved.

"Now get on your knees and suck my cock, you dirty slut."

She does as she's told and when she works her little fingers around my belt buckle; I lean back on the dingy bed. She's quick to pull me out of my pants, her need to be satiated filling the air around us. I know she's been worked up by Connor. I'm not stupid. I saw how they both looked. It doesn't matter to me though because I'll just finish what he started.

I lift my hips so she can pull down my pants and boxers, and when she's about to grab me in her small hand, I sink mine into her hair again.

"Now, I want you to fucking gag on this cock. Do you hear me?" She nods, but that's not what I want, so I yank on her hair and narrow my eyes at her.

"Yes, sir."

As soon as her warm mouth envelops my cock, I groan and drop my elbows back to the bed. Mary knows exactly what I like and soon enough, her gags are echoing throughout the room as my cock hits the back of her throat. She's working me with skill, but I can sense when the moment shifts and she needs something more.

I lean up and grab her hair, hauling her up to her feet to stand between my spread legs. "Take those clothes off." They're wet and clinging to her body. Her skin pebbled with the chill. I want her to warm up, and the only way it'll work is if we're skin-to-skin.

She quickly begins to strip, each piece of clothing hitting the floor with a wet *thunk*. Then she's standing in front of me completely naked as her hands stay fisted at her sides. She doesn't like to be scrutinized, but we're slowly changing that, and she knows I don't allow her to cover herself when she's alone with me.

I take off my clothes, tossing them to the floor next to hers, and then I motion for her to join me with a slow curl of my finger. A blush creeps along her chest and up over her throat before finally cascading across her cheeks in a beautiful, red hue.

"Ride this dick," I demand as she mewls. She straddles my waist and lines herself up, her eyes never wavering from mine. "I want to hear the sounds of your juices around this room."

She rides me fast and hard, her breathing coming in quick pants as her breasts heave with the motion. I lean forward and grab a dusty rose nipple between my teeth, grinning around the hardened nub when she squeaks. When I feel her pussy tighten, my hand seals around her throat, gripping her as I pull her closer to my face.

"Turn around and ride my cock. I don't want to see your whore face."

Her eyes roll back into her head as she bites down on her lip, her pussy beginning to pulsate. "James, please, I'm so close."

I pull her pussy off my cock as she whimpers from the loss, then I give her ass a swift slap, forcing her eyes open.

"Do as you're told, slut," I grit out between my teeth, my cock jerking with the forlorn look she gives me.

"Yes, sir," she gasps and turns around to sit back on my cock.

Her wet pussy grips me tight in its sheath as I wrap my hands around her hips to guide her exactly how I want her. I sit up straight, pressing my chest to her back and my lips to her ear, the lobe bouncing against my mouth with her movements.

"Who's going to come all over my cock?" I ask her. "Which filthy little slut is going to have her cunt filled with my cum?"

Mary

"Me," I beg. "Fill it up."

The same mixture of shame and desire courses through me, but the shame is not as potent as it once was. When James and I first started our lovemaking, I thought he would leave me for sure. It's not normal to want to feel like nothing during sex. It can't be normal to want to feel worthless while my body hits its highest ecstasy.

James makes me feel worthy despite what I need to get off though.

His chest hair tickles along my back as his mouth hits my shoulder, the touch gentle despite his harsh words. He knows exactly the right balance between making me feel like nothing and letting me know I am his everything.

He pushes his hips upward, his cock hitting deep inside me and slowly dragging back out, drawing me closer to that edge I so desperately seek. I need something more, more depraved, more degrading.

"Only whores can take a cock this large with ease, someone whose pussy has been fucked loose," he growls menacingly into my ear as my pussy clamps down around his *large cock.*

My head falls back to his shoulder as a low whine escapes my throat, rapidly turning into a garbled mess of his name. Sensations course over me as I fly over the edge, my hips jerking erratically as James' hands roughly grab onto my tits.

I'm just coming down when he shouts my name and shoots his load deep inside of me, my pussy still pulsing and milking him dry. He gently lifts me off and settles me on the bed beside him before reaching into one of the bags he carried in here. James pulls out a small hand towel and I smile at his forethought, knowing I would need it during our stay here.

He gently cleans me between my legs while murmuring sweet things, and then he pulls out one of his T-shirts to pull over my head. "Your bag must be in the other cabin with Nick and Connor." He smooths back my hair and kisses my forehead. "I'll get it in a bit. I have the bag with our blankets."

"I love you," I tell him as my eyes begin to close.

"What's your name?"

I wake up to the sound of James' voice, the words lined in fear. His form slowly comes into view as I shake the last vestiges of sleep from my mind. He's standing rigidly straight with only a pair of track pants on, his hands fisted at his sides and his body vibrating. With fear or anger, I can't tell which.

"Why are you here?" he demands as I slowly sit up.

Oh, god, I think to myself. *Please, not this again.*

He's talking to someone I cannot see or hear, and the hairs begin to rise along my arms. This must've been how he felt whenever I would talk to Secretary Mary from Belgrove.

"James?" I whisper as I swing my legs over the side of the bed, then cringe from the chill as I push aside the blanket, exposing my bare legs to the air. "What's happening?"

That's when I notice the rain pelting on the tin roof and the loud thunder rumbling above our heads, shaking the rickety cabin. This storm was not on the forecast when we checked it before coming out.

"It's okay, baby," James soothes me over his shoulder, his eyes wide with fear. "It's okay."

"Who're you talking to?" I question as I slowly stand on my feet and make my way to his side.

"It's Daniel," he says before his head snaps forward and he raises his hands in a placating manner. "Right, sorry, Danny." He turns to me, lowering his arms, with a surprised look on his face. "He says only his mother calls him Daniel. Am I fucking dreaming?"

"You can see him?" I ask as I look to the corner of the room where James was talking. "Can he tell us about what happened?"

"I can see how he died," James utters, his voice crippled with dismay. "His throat is slashed."

"He was murdered?" I gasp and James holds up a hand to me.

"He's telling me what happened," he tells me as he curls me into his bare chest, his heart pounding against my ear.

I feel James stiffen and a few gasps escape him as he stares blindly into the empty corner of the cabin, listening to a story meant for his ears only. I wait patiently for the answers we're here to seek and decide this would be the moment our viewers would want to see a live feed.

I rush back to the clothing discarded on the floor and pull James' phone from his pants pocket. When I see we have no more service, I groan. We knew this would be a possibility, and we warned our viewers that if this happened, we would take videos to upload later.

So that's what I do.

Just as the recording begins, James mutters, *oh no,* and I look up to find him with his hand over his mouth.

"What is it?" I prompt him as I come closer, making sure he knows he's being recorded.

Right away, James morphs into his Phantom Chaser role and says, "We are being visited by a Silent Night Theme Park employee, Daniel Harris, but he likes to be called Danny. I have been listening to him tell his story of the horror that happened on this very island. It's a story of neglect on the builder's part and what was very clearly a money grab from the beginning."

"Danny is a ghost," I speak into the phone as I scan the light across the room, ensuring the people know there's no one with us. "We are staying in his employee cabin and we found his belongings as well."

"He wants us to tell his mother what happened. He's worried about his little sister," James continues. "He says he wants justice for the hundreds of people who lost their lives here because, for a long time, he felt like it was his fault, but now he knows differently."

"Why did he think it was his fault?" I urge.

"What Connor said today beside the swing ride was accurate. The crank had jammed, and the ride was out of control. There was no stopping it. Danny says the sounds of children's screams still haunt him."

"Is he here alone?" My hands shake from the chill and the rain begins to drum harder on the roof. "Are there any others here on the island?"

For a few minutes, the only sounds around us are of the booming thunder and rain, but when James finally turns to look at me, his eyes shining with terror, I know I'm not going to like what I'm about to hear.

"Danny says the island is full of children looking for their parents and a few of the workers, but he says there's something worse lingering on the grounds and it's been terrorizing the spirits, keeping them trapped here."

"What?" My voice cracks as I stare back at him, the phone dropping to my side. "Another Conroy?"

"So much worse."

Nick

A light beams in from the outside, penetrating my eyelids. I stretch and try my best not to disturb Connor on this cot we migrated to last night. My heart is finally at peace knowing Connor is back in my arms where he belongs, but the heavy burden of knowing Conroy is still with us has a weight bearing down on my soul.

I've got to find a way to get the motherfucker gone and not let Mary or James know. They went through enough shit at his sick-ass hands. Well, I'm not exactly sure how my brother would react, but I'm not willing to chance it.

I stare at Connor's sleeping face a moment longer before my bladder screams at me to get up. Quietly, I ease out of the bed and walk outside to see a little bit of sunshine, but the gloomy clouds are rolling back in, so this piece of serenity is about to get nasty again.

I walk over to the overgrown bushes beside the cabin and unzip my jeans. Pulling my dick out, I yawn and freeze when the bushes rustle beside me. I don't have losing my cock to a lizard on my death bucket list, so I quickly try to stuff it back in, then yelp when I end up zipping some of the skin in the zipper. I try desperately to keep my scream muffled as vomit works its way up my throat.

"Damn, mister. That sure looks like it hurts," a small voice says, causing me to quickly turn around. I jerk my hips back quickly while snatching my pants forward and cry behind sealed lips when the skin parts from the metal bars of death. Thank fuck my piercings didn't get caught.

"Why is it, when my dick is out, you little shits seek me out?" I ask the little boy apparition in front of me. Billy definitely cursed me on his way to the other side if this is the shit I'm going to have to deal with every investigation we do. This kid looks a lot younger than Billy did, however. His little T-shirt is ripped and blood covers him in places, almost like he was permanently stuck in this form upon his death. His shorts look like they were tan at one point, but the horror that day the park faced is forever imprinted on him. He's also missing a shoe.

"I'm sorry. I just wanted to find my mommy. I'm scared and I don't know where I am," the boy responds before dropping his head to walk away.

Fuck my bleeding heart.

"Wait! I'm sorry. What's your name?" I kneel to his level and try to appear gentle.

"I'm Andy. I've had to hide a really long time and I think my mommy forgot about me." Even though I can almost see right through this kid, he looks like he has tears dripping down his face. Jane chooses that moment to appear as she yips happily, and I see the boy light up slightly when a smile pulls at his mouth. Jane walks over to brush against the boy but passes right through him, though I can tell just that one little act from Jane helps the scared kid.

"My name is Nick. Can you tell me why you're hiding?" I keep my hands in front of me on the ground so he doesn't feel threatened or startled.

"Because if he finds us, he eats us. He made sure to make everyone on the island stay here when he messed with the crank on the swing set." Andy speaks while petting Jane. Chills erupt all over my body as I listen to this little boy that's being tormented in his afterlife. I want to ask more questions but am quickly cut off. "I just want to find my mommy and go home," Andy whines, starting to whimper slightly. He wrings his hands in front of him while he kicks at the dirt with his one shoe that has holes in it. The dirt never moves as his little foot just passes right through it.

"It's okay. I'm going to help you," I tell him, wishing more than anything I could hug him.

"Oh, no... It's the other one," Andy whispers, his already translucent-self paling to the point he starts going invisible. I ask him what he means when he points over my shoulder. Turning around quickly, I see Connor watching me curiously. "He'll eat us too," Andy mutters before disappearing completely.

Connor

I tried to be as quiet as possible when I heard Nick talking outside. When I snuck around the corner, it was like the poor scared kid sensed me coming. Because of Conroy, I can see him and hear him as well. I know it was my fucking baggage that startled this boy into running.

"Wait, Andy! Come back!" Nick exclaims in a panic. The little boy reappears behind the bushes, keeping a healthy distance from me, and Nick breathes a sigh of relief at seeing him again. "I promise you, Connor won't hurt you. He's in control of himself," he promises, giving me a pointed look that causes my dick to twitch, remembering his orders from last night as he brought me to ruin.

Andy looks me up and down before nodding his head, but he stays behind the bushes, using them as a shield. I hear Conroy chuckle in my mind and I want nothing more than to punch his face in over it.

"At least the kid has good survival instincts if he knows to keep himself hidden from me," the bastard replies.

"We both know what you're really about, Conroy. You left that door open for me to look inside, remember?" I taunt him and get a snarl in reply before he goes silent. Maybe taking control of him was easier than I made it out to be because I don't feel him trying to command my body anymore.

"What do you mean by he eats you?" Nick asks Andy, drawing my attention back to them. Jane creeps up to the boy again, trying to offer comfort as her tongue lolls out of her mouth from the moist heat beating down on us.

"That's why he's so strong. He eats the other spirits on the island. It's like he's slurping soup and they sound so bad when he does it. Next thing I know, they're gone. I tried to look for them after that, but I can never find them," Andy explains as his bottom lip wobbles.

I feel physically sick from his explanation and I know Nick feels the same as I do when I see him grab his stomach.

"I'll tell you what, Andy. I need you to trust me, okay? I have an idea. It requires you to stick close to us, okay? I know Connor seems scary right now, but you said he was like the bad man, right? The secret is Connor isn't bad at all. He's a good guy and I trust him with my life. The bad man won't get you if you stay close to me and him, okay?" Nick holds out his hand to Andy even though Andy could never grab it, but I get the reassurance he's offering.

Can I protect this kid from Conroy? I feel like today is a brand new day on my journey and I feel stronger than before since Belgrove.

When Andy nods his little head again, I know for sure I have to do everything I can to make it so.

"Let's catch up with James and Mary." I put my hands in my pockets to try and appear as nonthreatening as possible, but it looks like this kid will never trust me in a million years. Not that I blame him. Nick stands and directs Andy to follow us as we head over to the next cabin.

Walking in the door, I see Mary looking terrified and James having a conversation with another spirit. Nick and I pause so as to not startle him too as the man freezes and looks me over.

Andy comes up beside me, wrapping a small arm around my leg even as it passes through slightly, stunning me completely.

"This one said he was a good guy. He'll keep the bad man away," Andy explains to the man as he narrows his eyes on me.

"You hurt him? I'll find a way to harm you back," the man growls, balling his fists up tight. James' head whips around, spotting us.

"What does he mean?" James asks. This is going to be hell.

"What who means?" Nick replies, tilting his head and looking around the cabin. So it seems only Nick can see small children while James is being haunted by this guy.

"Not important." James turns back around to face the man. "Continue explaining."

"I think I'll speak again when he isn't around, but I'll be close to keep an eye on you all," the man warns before disappearing completely.

James turns back around, looking pissed off as he eyes me. Nick grabs my hand and squeezes in silent support. James' features soften as he gives us a nod.

"It's about damn time. You two were driving us nuts," Mary says, drawing a laugh from us all. I squeeze Nick's hand again before walking over to her.

"I'm sorry about everything. I'll be better and in control from now on," I tell her, running my thumb along her jawline, watching as her eyes start to flutter shut.

"Now would be a good time to call her a dirty whore and fuck her," Conroy snips lustfully and I slam the door shut on him, blocking him out completely.

I hope I can keep this promise to her.

SIX

Mary

I want to go home.

None of this is fun anymore. When we first started Phantom Chasers, we were kids terrorizing the neighborhood in search of dead people. What started out as something fun and creepy is becoming all too real. I don't think any of us could've imagined just how real this would become. Meeting actual ghosts, conversing with them, running from them, being *fucked* by them.

Connor hauls me into his arms as I breathe in his familiar scent and soak up his warmth. There's nothing in this world quite as comforting as a hug from Connor. He has a way of enveloping you in a blanket of safety with just his powerful arms.

"Tell us about what happened in here," he says as his arms tighten around me and his nose lands on the top of my head. He's so different from the man he was yesterday and my heart tugs at knowing how hard of a time he's having to accept his feelings, knowing it's not what some would perceive as *normal*.

"James met the guy who was there the day everything went wrong. He was in charge of the swing ride." I pull back to look up at him, seeing confusion flicker across his features. "The one you were at yesterday, and his story sounds a lot like yours."

"It wasn't hard to figure out." He clears his throat and pulls back to look at a narrow-eyed James. "The crank was broken." He ends his explanation with a shrug as Nick stands beside him and begins to rub his back.

There's more to the story. I can see it in the guilty downcast look Connor has on his face and the way he can't bring himself to look at me, but I let it go. This isn't the time or place to begin a deep dive into the inner workings of Connor's mind. I will admit, they're more at ease this morning than they've ever been. Maybe they had a wild night too. My cheeks heat as my eyes land on James, finding him already looking at me with pure lust in his eyes.

"I think you guys have my bag in your cabin," I say to Nick. "I need my clothes and then we should head out to the park again to get some footage."

"Do we have service yet?" James asks as he takes his phone out of my hand. He grins and holds it in the air to wave his one bar around. "Better than nothing."

"I don't think it'll last long," Nick tsks. "There seems to be another storm coming in."

"I'll get your bag and be right back," Connor offers and heads out of the small cabin. I'm sort of glad as the space was beginning to feel a little too claustrophobic.

When Connor comes back with my bag, he and the brothers step out of the cabin and shut the door behind them, giving me a little privacy to change. At least we won't be spending another night here. I can get through the morning as long as I keep in mind we're leaving this afternoon.

"Hey, Danny?" I call out into the cabin, knowing I won't get a response, so I continue, "I need to get changed, so if you're in here, turn around. I know you've probably seen me with all three of them and even though they don't mind sharing amongst themselves, they will not like you watching. No more ghosts." I shudder as my mind flicks back to Belgrove and the night I was violated by Conroy. Only the shudder isn't solely out of disgust. I huff out my breath as I rip off James' T-shirt and grab my still-damp bra from the floor. It'll have to do because I didn't bring an extra one. "Why are you still on the island, Danny? Is there something you left unfinished? Maybe if it's only James who can see you, you should ask him what it is you need to cross over. Living here, even as a ghost, can't be fun." I pull on the rest of my clothes as thunder begins to rumble in the distance again. "Shoot."

"Mary!" Nick knocks on the door. "Let's get going. We need to get some live streaming done before this storm comes in."

That's when it really hits me. If there's another storm today, we may not be able to leave this island. That would mean being here another night here, and the thought has me whispering a prayer to whoever is listening to ensure that I'm not stuck in yet another ghost situation.

As soon as I step out, I see James with his phone recording and his hands moving animatedly as he no doubt tells our viewers a story of carnage. Nick says something about checking on our boat as another loud rumble sounds overhead, and I turn to find myself with Connor, his hands in his pockets as he kicks at the ground.

He's so different today, back to being the quiet boy I know so well, but I can't deny I miss the man who had me pressed up against a tree yesterday. A moan slips from between my lips, making Connor's head snap up and his eyes to meet mine. Whatever he sees in their depths has his mouth tipping up at the corner and his lids growing heavy.

"What?" he husks, his voice rough with desire.

"I was thinking about yesterday," I whisper and watch his eyes grow darker as his tongue slips out along his bottom lip. "How you were tasting me."

I can feel my cheeks heat with my confession, but I refuse to lie to any of them, and I'm not going to feel bad for wanting all three of them. I think I'm enough for them and surely they all know what it is I like by now, having heard James and me multiple times.

Connor takes a few steps toward me, his hand scrubbing down his face as his eyes rake over my body, as if seeing me for the first time. He's had me, been inside me, but it wasn't actually him. I know how he feels, but he has no idea how I feel.

My head turns just as James rounds the corner and disappears on the path toward the theme park.

"Are you worried he won't like us getting too close?" Connor asks, his voice low.

"No, not really. It's still something I have to get used to." I shrug.

"Would it be too much for me to ask you to drop those pants and turn around to grip that tree behind you? I've already forgotten what you taste like, and I'd like a reminder." His mouth is captured in a sinful smile as his eyes hold a hint of bashfulness.

I gasp at his directness tinged with a shy tone, so much more like my Connor, the one I know makes my stomach flutter and my heart to pick up in my chest. "Connor." I look around us. "What if Nick comes back?"

"Tell me you didn't like what was happening yesterday, the rush of being caught, and you know he would join in a flash." He's walking me back toward the tree, his chest stretching with confidence as his eyes shine with a challenge.

I did love everything that happened yesterday, and I remember in vivid detail exactly what it felt like to have Connor's mouth sucking on my pussy, so of course I want a repeat. My fingers dip into the waistband of my track pants as he twirls his finger, motioning for me to turn around.

"Hands on the tree, Mary," he says quietly. "I'll get these pants off for you."

He does get the pants off me and my panties as well, both of them pooling around my shoes as he pushes me forward and angles my ass in the air. I hear the grass rustle as he drops to his knees behind me when suddenly I'm hit with a shot of apprehension. He's going to taste James inside of me.

"Wait, Connor…"

I'm cut off as he runs his tongue up my slit and groans when my essence floods into his mouth. I'm wet, practically dripping and he's slurping me like I'm a slushie on a hot day. The sounds of him feasting on my pussy collides with my moans and pants, creating an arrangement of lust and heat.

When his finger breaches my asshole, I give a loud shout as my pussy clamps around his tongue, uncaring about the echoes bouncing back at us. I'm so close to cresting that wave, I can feel the coil in my stomach tightening, but this isn't enough to pull me under. I need more and I'm not sure how to ask for it.

"Connor, I need…" My words end on a strangled moan as he bites my clit. "I need…"

"I know, Mary," he says as he stands. "I'll try my best, but the things James says, I don't know…"

His words trail off as I hear his pants come undone and turn to look at him over my shoulder. I see his happy trail of dark hair leading from his belly button down into his underwear, the same underwear he's shoving down to release his cock. It stands proud in the palm of his hand, the thick veins pulsing just beneath what I know is going to be the most velvet-feeling skin.

"Yes," I whisper, as I wiggle my ass. "Fuck me, Connor."

My mouth practically waters at the sight of him, and my pussy clenches with anticipation.

"Spread those legs as far as you can," he husks out. "I want this pussy to take every inch of me, and if she doesn't, your ass will."

There it is.

James

I grin as I enter the theme park, knowing exactly what it is Mary and Connor are doing back at the cabins. They need this time together. Connor needs to know we're here for the long run and no matter how he's feeling, we're not going anywhere.

Her shout echoes across the space between us and I chuckle as I imagine Connor plowing into her, my own cock hardening at the thought. Once I'm out of earshot, I take a deep breath and turn the phone back to face me, putting a smile on my face for the choppy video I'm trying to stream.

"The weather is acting up here, guys, but I promise, whatever I can't stream, I'll post videos of as soon as we get off this island." I steadily swing the phone back around and kick aside some brush as I enter the park. "Yesterday we showed you the swing ride and the destruction surrounding it, but today, I think I'll take you through what they called the village. It was built to look like little huts in the North Pole, and each hut was a game stand. Ball and Bucket Toss." I point the camera at the ragged-looking hoops still lining the wall inside the hut. "Balloon and Dart," I say as I walk by the next one.

This side of the park was relatively preserved, save for some holes gouged out of the sides of the huts, but all in all, it was abandoned with everything left behind. Large stuffed animals hang from hooks, their fur matted by the weather and their eyes hanging by threads.

"There was no time to collect belongings or to close the hut's shutters. They needed to run to save their lives." Even as I say the words with nothing but the sound of the strengthening wind around me, I can hear the screams, the cries, and the pleading with god to save them. I can hear the crash of metal and the booming of collapsing structures. I can smell burning metal, blood, and rain. I can sense all of it as if I were standing in the center of the madness, watching as everything around me exploded. "Let's head into the Duck Pond game, well, here it was the Penguin Ice Pod game." I lift the rickety counter, holding my breath as the hinges protest the movement after laying dormant for over fifty years. The inside of the hut is dark as shadows dance along the corners, and it smells of dampness and mold, but the place is still in pretty good shape. The stuffed animals are nearly coming apart at the seams, but it's amazing they're still attached to the hooks.

"Time has stood frozen on this island," I continue my story as I run my fingers over the small counter, the pads collecting grime. "And here, inside these little huts, we may uncover some secrets of what happened leading up to the disaster."

My phone begins to beep as the signal slowly fades and I curse as I place the phone on the counter. I'll continue taking videos for them to see what I unearth, but first, I pull the map out of my pocket along with the pencil I found on Danny's dresser. As soon as my fingers meet the wooden stick, I swear a jolt of energy spreads up my arm, making the hairs stand up straight.

"Fucking pussy," I grit out to myself as I trace the path I've taken on the map. I don't want to get fucking lost, and I told Nick I would meet him back at the front of the park in an hour. He wanted to explore more of the ride side together. He's always been one who loved to pick apart the mysteries of death. I like to tell the stories.

The wind gusts inside the hut, filled with humidity and warmth, making my face break out with perspiration. I can practically smell the storm in the current and curse under my breath as I slip the pencil and map back into my pocket. I need to record this shit and meet Nick before the rain hits.

As the small space around me decreases in temperature, I reach for the phone. The chill sends goose bumps along my skin as I gradually spin around. It's as if the wind completely stops and a bubble forms around the hut, effectively shutting off all sound. I exhale a breath and startle when it forms a white plume in front of my face.

"What the fuck?" I hiss and that's when a shadow shifts in the right corner, my eye just catching the slight movement. "Who's there?" I try to sound strong but my voice shakes as it shifts again, only this time two eyes begin to emerge.

I blink, willing it all to be a part of my imagination, but when I stare into that corner, those eyes become clearer. Pale blue irises appear from the shadows' darkest depth, the glossy orbs shining with a menacing mirth.

"This isn't real," I mutter, but I know better than to play it off as a trick of the mind. Not too long ago, I was having a conversation with a ghost.

Those eyes blink, a slow, dramatic close of the lids, the skin translucent and blue-veined. The lashes look gray, or blond, I can't tell, but when the lids open again, those eyes remain trained on my face.

"What do you want?" It comes out in a hoarse whisper as my stomach flips and my neck tingles with fear. "Who are you?"

The sound of a foot shuffling along the wood-planked floor has me sucking in a breath, readying to scream if need be. My pride quickly exits my body, replaced with the threat of my bladder control.

A jingle sounds and my eyes slip up to see a silver bell stitched into the tip of a Santa's hat sitting on top of the ghost's head of white-blond hair. The strands look stringy and limp; the ends tinged with red. Blood, I would assume. The assumption is confirmed when he shuffles forward again and I see his ear is missing, along with a large chunk out of the side of his head. My stomach rolls with nausea as I swallow to keep myself from spewing.

"Oh, yeah. That's a fine grade of lead right there." His voice sounds choppy and coarse, the tone gravelly and low. "All that fresh, unshaved wood. God, it probably smells like the forest." He takes an audible breath, the sound like a whistle as it flows through him.

His hand reaches forward, the knuckles gnarled and twisted, and a few fingers missing. He tugs on my pocket as I stand frozen in fear, unable to move a muscle. He's a fucking Santa Claus, decked out in the full suit, even if it is saturated and dripping in ghostly blood.

71

I let out an ungodly, girlish scream as he does the same, seemingly startled by my reaction.

"Holy fuck, can you see me?" he asks in shock, pulling back his hand.

"Santa?!" The name slips from my lips in the only response I can think to give him.

"The name's Peter, but unfortunately, when you lose your damn heartbeat, you're pretty much stuck in what you got on. Say, that's a fine-looking pencil in your pocket." He points down at my dick and I have the sudden urge to sock Santa right in his fucking face.

"You better back the fuck up," I order.

"No, kid. The pencil, not your dick. You freaks these days, I swear," he replies, face-palming himself, only his hand goes right through his features.

I look down and exhale another breath. Right, he means the actual pencil in my pocket. "What happened here?"

"What does it look like, kid?" He shakes his head, making the bell jingle once more. "You lost your peepers or somethin'? This is what happens when you take your investors' money, use a fraction of it to build the most dangerous theme park, forgetting building code and safety, and then you disappear with the rest, leaving a trail of death behind you like the Grim Reaper himself."

The ghost Santa slips back into the shadows, his voice becoming fainter as he continues to mumble about wood and the forest. Then soon enough, I'm alone once again. I grab up my phone as the wind pummels against the side of the hut and I let out a curse. I need to meet up with Nick and get back to the cabins.

I slip out of the hut as quickly as I can, glimpsing over my shoulder every few seconds, hoping I'm not being followed.

Nick

Thankfully, the boat is undamaged and intact despite the storm from last night. Hopefully, the one rolling in now won't do anything to our only means of leaving this place.

I sit on the dock and stare out at the gray mass in the sky sweeping toward us as the booming thunder rattles my bones and the crack of lightning across the sky blinds me from everything else but its powerful strike.

Fucking Conroy escaped with us at Belgrove. I don't know how he did it, but I'm starting to think it was my fault. If I hadn't demanded Billy be sent to the other side, the patient count would have stayed the same. But I would have lost Connor then. It's an absolute mind fuck to deal with. I will figure out a way to get that sick bastard gone. That's one thing I do know for sure.

Mary's cry of pleasure reaches my ears as a pause in the thunder silences the world around me. I grin as I stand, wiping the grime from the dock off my pants. There's not much investigating we're going to be able to do while this storm rages. Looks like we're going to be stuck here another night.

I start making my way back toward the cabins, noticing Andy following me from a distance as he carries on a conversation I can't quite hear. I assume it's with James' visitor because I don't see any worry or fear coming from him. Only ease and a familiar comfort. I've got to keep my promise to him as well and find his mom somehow.

As I approach the sounds of Connor's heavy breathing, I see Andy has disappeared completely, which is a good thing. Connor has Mary gripping a tree as he thrusts into her with abandonment, not caring who hears or sees them.

"Well, looks like our little resident whore is enjoying herself." I know exactly what gets Mary hot after some nights spent listening to her and James through the thin walls of our apartment. Mary freezes and swings panicked eyes toward me before releasing a guttural moan when Connor slaps her ass and orders her to keep her eyes on the ground. "Dirty little sluts don't get to look at us. They just get used for their holes. Isn't that right?" I taunt her, easing up beside her and leaning against the tree as Connor continues to plow into her. "Answer me, girl," I say, keeping my voice low but demanding.

"Yes, sir," she pants out back to me, still keeping her eyes on the ground. Sweat drips down Connor's face as he concentrates on chasing his pleasure. Watching him with Mary is too much for my poor aching cock to take, but I'm slightly gun-shy after my piss this morning. A smile stretches on my face as I reach down and free myself to pump my steel length.

"I got a boo-boo this morning, Mary. Want to kiss it better for me? I'm sure you don't mind a good spit roast, would you?" I slap her cheek a couple of times with my dick, waiting for her to turn her mouth toward me. When she complies, I grip the back of her hair and choke her on my cock when she screams.

"Fuck, she's gripping me like a vise right now. I can barely move," Connor moans. I look down and see the tears streaming down her face as drool runs down my shaft and off her chin. Her beautiful eyes stare at me with so much lust and excitement that I almost lose my load right then and there.

"Fuck," I wheeze out as I drop my head back against my shoulders and look at the dark sky above us. Connor's motion moves her mouth on me while she uses her tongue to play with my piercings. The first drops of rain start to come down and Mary takes me fully to the back of her throat. I can't hold on any longer. I tighten my grip on her hair and hold her to me as she struggles for air, relishing in the pulse of my cock as my orgasm grips me. Connor stills behind her, breathing just as heavily as I am.

Pulling out of her mouth, I gently lift her up as she drops to the ground before looking around for a place to clean her up. I see a faucet on the side of the cabin and carry her to it as I kiss her forehead softly.

"Do you know how amazing you are, Mary? I know you have your tastes, but one of these days I'm going to show you how good it feels to be cherished in bed. Maybe I'll even tie you and Connor up together and have my wicked way with you both," I tell her gently. She chuckles and blinks her tired eyes at me with so much love that I actually freeze for a moment.

"I think we aren't getting any water from this faucet, but there's a pitcher pump behind the cabin!" Connor says excitedly, bringing my attention back to him. I follow him to the back of the cabin and see what looks like an old-time wash station set up with a hand pump for water.

Connor gives the pump a couple of cranks as the rain starts coming down harder and rusty-looking water flows from the spigot.

"Hey, we can clean up later. Let's get inside before we catch a cold or something."

"That's a fucking myth, dude, but let's go." Connor laughs and follows along.

Connor

When we get in the cabin, we start stripping clothes off and grab dry ones. Nick towels Mary off as best as he can and dresses her before laying her down. She really is amazing, just like Nick told her. I walk over and kiss her head sweetly as her eyes flutter shut.

"Did you see which way James went? He should be back by now," Nick asks, and I shake my head. I was so wrapped up in Mary that I wasn't even paying attention if a snake was ready to bite me on the ass. "Shit! I was supposed to meet him at the rides, but then I heard you and Mary and completely forgot our plans!" Nick exclaims, a panicked look in his eyes.

"You stay with her. I'll go look for him," I tell him. He grabs my arm to stop me with a refusal on the tip of his tongue, but I hold a finger up to silence him. "I have a secret weapon, remember? You can protect her here. I won't be long," I assure him and give him a quick kiss before running out into the pouring rain.

"Secret weapon, huh? I thought I was just a sick bastard," Conroy pipes up and I roll my eyes.

"You are a sick bastard, but you seem to be of use for now, so don't get comfortable." Being in control this long feels so unusual since Conroy overtook me. I wonder if this is a new game he's playing or if I actually am in charge like Nick said.

"I'll repeat your words back at you, little boy, don't get too comfortable. You gave me some of Mary's sweet pussy, so I'm content for now, but don't fucking push your luck," he says, before fading slightly.

I jog at a steady pace as the storm rages around me, only struggling in places here and there to get through the brush. It's times like this when Jane would come in handy if she had the proper training. She'd be able to find James in an instant. I haven't seen her since this morning with Andy, however. Now I'm worried about the fucking mutt.

A growling noise has me turning and squinting through the downpour. Speaking of mutts, I see Jane crouched over James' body as she snarls and snaps at something I can't hardly see other than a black mass.

"JAMES!" I scream as I run toward him. The vines and tree limbs trip and slap at me as I fight the storm and the overgrowth.

"Let me the fuck out now, Connor! NOW!" Conroy demands, beating at the cage of my mind. I close my eyes and let his darkness take over.

Conroy

Connor's urgency bleeds into our bones as I race against mother nature to save this fucking dickhead's life. I'm more alert now that I know exactly what the fuck this thing is and if I don't get there in time, James is going bye-bye.

Honestly, I don't really give a fuck, but I can't have these jackasses moping over his corpse. Sexy time just won't be so sexy then. I hear Connor huff even with panic crippling his senses.

Busting through the last of the brush, I release a snarl myself as the poltergeist turns to look at me. I don't even spare James a glance as I keep my eyes trained on the smoky darkness in front of me.

"I said, these are mine now. You don't listen too well." I know this fucker can hear and understand me as we spoke just yesterday.

It sends out a stream of smoke that passes right through me. I don't feel anything, but Connor cries out in agony. When the trail returns to the demon, it seems to savor it.

"How do you have essence, but no essence?" it hisses.

"Because I'm the fucking devil," I growl, now extremely pissed the fuck off. If Connor dies, I lose this corporeal flesh and can't enjoy all the pleasures it offers.

It hisses at me again before it vanishes and I rush over to James. He's so pale, I actually get slightly concerned he may be dead. I toe him with my shoe and relax a little when he groans.

"Oh, thank fuck. Mary will suck my dick for being a hero again. I just know it this time," I say out loud, really giddy.

"Could you be less fucking perverted?" Connor snaps and then groans in pain.

"The fuck is wrong with you?" Again, I really don't care, but it seemed like a natural question to ask.

"I don't know. Whatever it did, I feel like I was put through a meat grinder," Connor replies.

I pick James up and heave him over my shoulder. It's slow going to make my way back to the cabins as the heavy rain starts creating the worst, muddy obstacles for me while carrying this heavy asshole. Jane yips happily by my side, not caring one fucking bit about the weather.

As soon as I reach the cabin and carry James inside, Mary is awake and both she and Nick start to grow anxious. I'm not good at emotions, so I set James down and release my hold on Connor.

SEVEN

Connor

The shift happens so suddenly that I stumble. Nick catches me as Mary drops to the floor, checking over James. Every inch of my body fucking hurts. I don't know what that thing did to me, but that was only a taste of whatever transpired with James.

"What happened?" Nick asks in a panic. He's so torn between checking on me and checking on James that he looks like he's about to faint. It's barely hit noon, but the heavy storm outside makes it look like nighttime.

"Poltergeist," I manage to wheeze out as my legs finally give out and I land hard on my ass. Mary's gasp has us focusing directly on James as she pulls up his soaking-wet shirt to see countless scratches crisscrossing his flesh. There are even bite marks on his side. Mary touches them gently, drawing a groan out of James as he moves around. Blinking his eyes open, he winces hard at the pain he's in.

"Fuck. That hurt," he says in a whisper. His head lops toward me and he mouths thank you. How the hell he knew it was me that saved him is beyond me right now.

"Let's get them laid down in the beds to rest. As soon as this storm passes, we're getting the fuck off this island," Nick orders as he moves to Mary and they work together to get James undressed and in the cot. Mary heads outside with a towel she pulls from one of the bags, her frantic energy pouring through the room. When Nick moves over to help me up, I wave him off.

I manage to pull myself up off the floor before Nick starts to help me undress as well. Mary tends to James, trying her best to clean the mud and cuts on him with the towel she wet from outside.

"This isn't natural, man. This is something else we aren't prepared for," Nick mutters, scanning me over. Instead of letting him, I grab his arm and pull him down to sit on my lap with his knees straddling me. Cupping his cheek, I give him a gentle kiss.

"We can't give up. You promised, Andy. We can't just leave these souls to suffer. There's got to be another way." Nick's features soften at my words and he drops his head to my shoulder as I hug him tightly to me. "Let's go grab some beds from the other cabins and push them together. I think we could all use a nap," I suggest, and he nods his head.

My body still feels like hell, but I need to be strong right now because losing my shit will only make this situation worse.

"So you really don't have control over me, do you? You just let me think you did," I ask Conroy, the question that's been bugging me since we saved James.

"The mind is a powerful place. It's the single, greatest weapon that can be molded and manipulated however you want it to be. You find a weak fool, or a sheep that follows the mob, and they can be played like a finely-tuned guitar," Conroy mutters around a yawn. I guess flexing whatever powers he has takes a toll.

When Nick is ready, I grab his hand and venture back into the storm with him. Hopefully incident-free this time.

James

Pain radiates through my body as a roar of thunder shakes the cabin. I don't know how long I've been out, but this storm is still raging on. There's heat in front of me and behind, and I feel like I've been stuffed into a can like a sardine. I crack open my eyes to see a sleeping Mary in front of me; her face riddled with worry even in sleep. I slowly lift my head and look over my shoulder to find my brother with his back to me and cradling a sleeping Connor. I'm about to question how the hell we're all on a single cot when I noticed they lined up three.

I chuckle, knowing they had to pull them from the other cabins, refusing to keep us separated, and then the pain hits again. With it comes a torrent of memories of what happened before Connor found me.

I left that hut and headed toward the rides, but my skin was pebbling with electricity. I remember looking around me, trying to see if that creepy fucking Santa had followed me, but I could hardly make out my surroundings through the rain.

When I felt the need to find my brother, I picked up the pace. The rain stopped, but only in a three-foot radius around me, and only because something was standing in front of me. Black smoke billowed out of a crack in the ground, its swirling mass slowly forming into a figure.

The roar of the thunder was drowned out by the booming chuckle emanating from the thing in front of me, its height well above me by a few feet. I tipped my head back as I swallowed down my fear, then thoughts of my brother slammed into me. I couldn't have Nick stumble upon this, not when he was still so fragile after what happened at Belgrove. As his big brother, it was up to me to protect him.

So that's when I turned on my heel and ran. Or at least tried to. I remember being lifted off the ground by my feet, my head swinging dangerously close to the concrete. I opened my mouth to scream, only to have it filled with acrid, black smoke, the burn coursing its way down my throat. It felt like I was being fed molten lava, and my insides were scorched as it slowly pushed its way inside me.

That's when I knew I was being possessed. So I fought.

I held my breath, forcing my mouth shut, and biting down on the smoke inside of me. Heat pummeled against my lips, but I refused to open them for fear I would be lost forever. Or worse, stuck on this island for the rest of my life. That must've been close to what Connor felt back at Belgrove, and I all of a sudden knew exactly why he was so fucking scared.

My body is dropped with force and the rain once again began to pelt down over me as I opened my mouth to take a breath, and watched with wide, fearful eyes as a plume of black smoke escaped from between my lips.

Unfortunately, that's not where it ended. This thing didn't like being told no, and even worse, it didn't like it from a weak human.

"Get on your feet." The sound of its voice was like nothing I had ever heard before. Something akin to grinding gears and scraping metal, but somehow the phonics came through. I could understand it.

I rolled onto my back, my eyes pinched shut from the pain of my insides, and that's when I felt it. A warm breath rolling over my drenched face, the scent like sulfur and acid. Heat seeped through my soaked clothing, straight to my skin, the feeling like a warm embrace.

Slowly, I opened my eyes, the heat making them water instantly, distorting the view, but as I blinked them away, the black cloud above me took shape.

A large hood encased an elongated head, the orbs of its eyes were a coal-black without a bit of white, and there, nestled in the center, was a bright red pupil. Open sockets cushioned the orbs without lids, and the middle of its face had a gaping hole where our noses sit. The mouth was like melted skin; the smoke dripping off the lips like globs of darkened flesh.

I opened my mouth to scream, or maybe to gasp. I can't be sure, but it took that opportunity to try and once again to take me over. That time, I rolled onto my stomach and clamped my mouth shut as I dug my fingertips into the concrete to haul myself away.

I was no match.

I was lifted from the ground and thrown back down, the continuous impact like boulders against my body. I tried to stay conscious, to fend off his attack, but by the third blow to my head, I felt myself starting to sink into a dark abyss. The final time I hit the ground, I felt it move over me; the heat rolling over my skin as sharp objects punctured the surface. I had no voice left, no will to fight, and I was just about to give up when I heard my name being called.

Then Connor was there, his face an angry mask of fury, only it didn't look like Connor. His features were wrong, older, and slightly demonic.

I turn once more, hissing through the pain to look at Connor's sleeping face, trying desperately to see what I saw before, but it's not there. He's just Connor. I settle back onto the makeshift, king-sized bed to find Mary looking at me through tired, wary eyes.

"Hey," she whispers, her voice filled with apprehension.

"Hi," I croak out, my throat still feeling like it's on fire.

She reaches behind her and pulls out one of the water bottles we brought onto the island and my mouth salivates through the extreme thirst. I gulp down the bottle and moan through the instant relief, the cool liquid soothing the burn.

"What happened, James?" Her eyes fill with tears as her small hand settles on my cheek, her cool skin like a balm.

"We need to get off this island." As I say the words, my stomach rolls with fear. That thing is still here somewhere. "There's this thing, not a ghost, maybe a demon—"

"It's been here since before the theme park." Danny's words have me jolting upward, the pain making me cry out as Mary startles and wraps her hands around my arm.

"What's happening?" Nick groans groggily as Connor stirs.

"Danny's here," I detail to them as I wince and sit up. "He's telling me about the thing that lives here." I motion for Danny to continue as his eyes stray over to Connor curiously.

"As I was saying, that thing was here long before we came. Workers died building this place, freak accidents happened all the time, and the owners just ignored it all. We knew there was a curse, but we were contractually bound to this island, unable to leave." He begins to pace at the end of our bed, his feet shuffling over the dusty floor.

"What's he saying?" Nick asks me as his arm snakes around Connor's shoulders.

I can see Connor's eyes following Danny's movements, making it obvious he can see him too, but for some reason, I don't call him out on it. He's been through enough with seeing ghosts. I don't want to force him into another situation.

"He's telling me about the thing that attacked me," I explain and nod to Danny to carry on.

"We watched as our friends burned from unexplained fires, fell from heights as if being pushed, and we all lived in fear of what would happen next. The curse changed us. We no longer left our cabins when the sun set, and a group of us had a plan to sneak off with the next supply shipment. Only that was after the park's opening day. The following day, to be exact. We only had to survive one day of customers, one day of a filled resort, and then we would be free. Obviously, that didn't happen because *he* knew our plans. So he made sure we could never leave and now he spends his days haunting the dead."

"He says this island has always been haunted by that thing, by *him*," I inform the others as Danny heads for the door.

"I need to check up on Andy," he exclaims as he raises his hand. "You guys will be fine here with him protecting you." He juts his chin toward Connor, then disappears through the door.

"What does he mean by saying Connor will protect us?" I ask as I look around Nick to Connor.

"Probably because he's the one who saved you from that thing," Nick says as he bends and kisses Connor's cheek, the peaks turning crimson under our scrutiny. "But I should've been there, James. I'm so sorry."

"Where were you?" I ask, my attention solely focused on Nick now. "What happened?"

"He heard me and Connor," Mary cuts in, her voice ladened with sadness. "It's my fault all this happened, because of my stupid need to be—"

"Stop," I interject. "None of this was your fault."

"I just want you guys all the fucking time," she growls and strikes the cot with her small fists. "I'm sick."

Nick groans at her words, and I begin to grow hard at the thought of her and Connor. Maybe we're all sick. I can't deny how much I like the way she needs us, all three of us, or how she's the glue keeping our group together.

That's the thought swirling through my head when I lean in and frame her pretty face with my hands. "Don't do that," I grind out, hoping she can hear the sincerity in my voice. "Don't blame yourself. We each want you to feel loved and protected, and you deserve it."

A sob climbs from her chest and escapes her mouth as I press my lips to hers, swallowing the sob and letting it settle in my chest. I'll forever take her pain if it means she'll be free of the despair that's lived inside of her for years. I'll help shoulder her shame if it means she feels freer and safe.

"Since James is sore," I hear Nick say with a quick chuckle.

"Maybe we'll let him lay back while we take care of Mary. What do you think, Connor?"

"I think I wouldn't mind round two," Connor chimes in.

"I'm not sitting out for nothing," I snap, and then let loose a laugh at the confusion on Mary's face. "But I wouldn't mind watching for a bit."

Mary

I'm not sure how we got to this point, but as I look from face to face at the three boys I've loved nearly my entire life, I feel nothing but adoration and acceptance. It both overwhelms and confuses me. Why do they love me so wholeheartedly? What did I ever do to deserve such a reward?

"Looks like she's lost inside her head again," Nick muses as he crawls over his brother to fist his T-shirt he dressed me in and drags me over James to him. "Looks like my girl needs a reminder of what she means to us." Then he lowers his voice as his tongue darts out to skim across my lips and says, "Of what she means to me."

"Nick," I mutter as my voice wavers with emotion and my hands wrap around his wrist. "I'm so scared," I admit.

James' hand skims up the back of my thigh and under the shirt to graze along my ass cheek while Nick leans forward to suck my bottom lip into his mouth, his teeth nipping the flesh. *Is this really happening?* As Nick finally takes my mouth in a soul-wrenching kiss, my eyes are open and watching Connor as he watches me kiss his boyfriend.

First, his cheeks bloom with a red hue as his eyes narrow in on us, then his chest begins to pump fast with each breath. The groan that escapes him sounds tortured and filled with longing even though he just had me a mere few hours ago.

James and I moan simultaneously as his fingers discover I'm not wearing panties, and he rubs through my folds as I kiss his brother.

"Take out your cock, Nicky," he orders his brother. "Stroke it while I stroke her. Connor," he turns his head to pin Nick with a glare. "Come taste her asshole while I finger fuck her wet pussy." Connor gets off the bed with little convincing and the rest of us shift downward to make room. Nick makes quick work of his pants and my mouth waters at the sight of his thick cock springing forward, his piercing on display. He and I have messed around, but I haven't had him inside of me yet, and my pussy clenches with anticipation. "Brother, her pussy appreciates the view," James cuts in, his eyes on his brother's cock. "Give her a bit more of a show, then stuff her filthy mouth with it."

I feel the rush of wetness coat my thighs at the words tumbling from James' mouth, and even though he's not as active as the rest of us, he's showing us just how in charge he is.

Connor crawls behind me and I feel him lift the shirt up over my ass as James finally sinks two fingers deep into my core. Nick strokes his cock, the veins on his arms flexing as he tips his head to the side, wanting to watch as Connor spreads my ass cheeks.

"Looks like Nick wants to watch his boyfriend fuck your asshole with his tongue, baby," James coos. "Should we let him? You want to be my good little slut and let Nicky watch you be used?"

"Yes," I cry out as Connor's breath and James' fingers drive me nearer to that edge. "Yes, Nick, please."

"Nick," James says without taking his eyes off of me. "Stick your cock in her mouth and make her gag."

Nick rises to his knees in front of me as James continues his rhythmic thrusting with his fingers, and then I feel Connor's hot breath on my asshole. The pierced tip of Nick's cock hits my lips and I immediately open them on a moan, my stomach quivering with the pent-up energy coiling in its depths.

The first dip of Connor's tongue has me crying out around Nick's cock, the sound cut short when he thrusts down my throat. My ass cheeks are spread to the point of pain, the velvet feel of Connor's tongue soothing the sharp ache. James continues his assault on my cunt, the sounds embarrassingly loud in the small cabin. Everything feels too much. Too much sensation, too much stimulation, too much depravity, but I never want it to stop.

"Connor," James grits out between his teeth as his eyes stay trained on Nick's cock in my mouth. "Tell me how that asshole tastes."

"So fucking good," Connor groans, then dives back in between my cheeks.

His tongue penetrates my tight ring of muscle, the stretch always so deliciously painful. My ass is used to being stretched by James, especially when he's lost in the moment of our immorality.

"Look how pretty you are being fucked in every hole, the perfect little slut," James praises me and I lose my vision as my eyes roll back in my head.

"She's so fucking perfect," Nick grounds out as he continues to fuck my mouth, his balls hitting against my chin.

I flatten my tongue around Nick's length and hollow out my cheeks to cushion every inch of him. My jaw is growing tired from accommodating his size, and my eyes grow blurry as tears well up around my lids. I'm fighting for each breath as my mouth waters, anticipation coating every moan. I want to be fucked in every hole and at the same time.

I reach my hand down between James and I to grip his cock through his pants. He gasps and thrusts upward, only to hiss when the movement causes him pain. I release Nick's cock and grip it with my other hand as I look down into James' face, his features saturated with torment.

"Are you okay?" I ask him as his eyes snap open and narrow on me.

"That whore mouth should be filled with a cock," he snarls. "Nick, must I show you everything?"

Then I watch with astonishment as James grabs his brother's throbbing cock, gives it a long, sure stroke, then guides it toward my open mouth. Nick curses under his breath, probably from the feel of his brother's rough hand and the fact that it's his brother touching him so intimately.

It takes our depravity to a whole new level, and I can barely keep it together as I tumble off the edge of bliss, my body quaking from the impact, with Nick's cock in my mouth, James' fingers in my cunt, and Connor's tongue in my ass.

EIGHT

Nick

James doesn't let go. Even with Mary's sweet mouth wrapped around me, he doesn't stop stroking me.

Belgrove flashes through my mind and I chance a glance at Connor behind Mary. He's focused on his task and only has eyes for her ass right now. James leans over Mary and gets close to my ear.

"You see how beautifully she comes for us? Shut off your mind and just feel, little brother," he whispers quietly. I look at him and notice the gleam of mischief in his eyes. He leans over further and kisses the corner of my mouth so softly that I finally close my eyes and shut off my brain like he's asked. I focus only on feeling. "Connor, let's move this little whore around," I hear James demand as I'm shoved back against the cot and something covers my eyes. I feel my arms wrenched above me and get tied to the bedposts as well.

"What—" I start, but stop when I feel a pair of lips come down on top of mine as a very tiny feminine body straddles me. I know it's Mary cause those tits brush against my chest as I devour her.

A hand grips my length, causing me to hiss out, and Mary lowers her tight little cunt down on me. When she gets settled and her pussy is gripping me like a vise, I feel the pressure of someone else, filling her ass through that little thin layer.

"Fuuuuuck," I moan when whoever is taking her ass starts to move and ends up massaging me as well.

"Jesus, I'm so full," Mary groans and then gasps.

"You don't get to speak when you're servicing us," James tells her roughly and I guess he shoves his cock in her mouth because the only thing I hear from her after that is a lot of muffled moans.

"I can feel you through her," Connor rumbles from above us, and goddamn if his sex voice doesn't make me want to come on the spot. Mary clenches around me as I start thrusting from the bottom.

I'm not going to last. I can't grab her hips as I struggle to fight my bindings. I plant my feet on the bed and start at a furious pace to vent my frustration. I want to feel skin smacking skin, but this will have to do.

Connor starts losing his rhythm as I feel drool pooling on my chest from James using Mary's mouth. Mary clenches down on me again, screaming out her release, and James follows, shouting out his.

Connor and I tag team Mary, pumping in and out without coordination until he ceases up and I feel the tingle in my balls. Throbbing inside her as I groan, Mary leans down and kisses me again. I can taste the saltiness of my brother on her tongue, but for once, I don't think, I just kiss her senselessly without a care in the world.

My arms are still tied above my head and the blindfold is in place when I feel Mary drop down beside me, sighing contentedly as the guys get up.

"Think you could help me out here, Mary?" I ask, putting my best helpless pouty look on. She snorts and then starts to giggle as I feel something wet lapping at my balls.

"Fuck, Connor, stop! I just got off, man. Those berries are sensitive!" I wiggle, trying to get away from the onslaught attacking me. I freeze when a cold nose connects with my ass and Jane yips happily. "Fucking shoo! Nasty mutt!" I yell as Mary and the guys burst out laughing. Connor finally shows me mercy and undoes my bindings, dropping down beside me to snuggle in as James crawls up on Mary's other side.

Conroy

As soon as Connor's head hits the pillow, it's lights out. I don't blame the dude. That was one hell of an orgy. I think I might enjoy sticking around with these kids if this is what our extracurricular nights will look like. Count me the fuck in.

I'm about to turn into little Mary and stick Connor's dick in her again when I hear a throat clear. With a groan, I look around the cabin and find that annoying ghost who almost had his head severed off by a chain. Poor way to go.

Not that I had it any better.

"What do you want?" I ask him with a roll of my eyes. "Can't you see I had an eventful night? I need rest."

"We both know you weren't the one in the middle of that," the shit says with a grin. "How did you tag along inside of him?"

His question both makes me feel superior—because I am—and wary. He's not asking out of mild curiosity, he's asking because he wants to hop into one of these kids' bodies. That won't happen on my watch.

"Listen, asshole," I start as I roll to the side of the cot and stand, letting him see Connor in all his naked glory. "You go ahead and try to slip into one of their bodies." I pop my neck. "It's been a while since I've violated a kid."

The smirk falls from his face and I watch as his slit throat works on a ghostly swallow. Some human reactions remain even in death. When he shakes his head and drops his shoulders, I can see the defeat emanating off of him in thick waves.

"I just want to get off this island. We're trapped here with that thing," he spits out. "He won't let us leave, and his favorite pastime is to torture us. He's always saying we don't put up much of a fight."

"Well, why don't you put up a fight?" I sneer. "It's not like you can die again."

"He'll consume us." His words are now filled with fear as he stares at me with wide eyes. "When someone fights against his torture, he eats them. They disappear."

I begin to get dressed as my mind reels with what it is they're dealing with here on the island. Something which can consume souls, inflict torture on both human and ghosts, and possesses an energy filled with evil.

"This isn't a regular poltergeist," I mumble as I pull the shirt over my head. "Tell me more about what you know."

The sounds of the rain have died down, the *pitter-patter* of the drops slowing and I can't hear any more thunder. Looks like my feet are going to be soaked from the wet grass because I'm going to need to find this thing and give him a proper fight.

"He said this was his island until we came with bulldozers and started building. He said we disturbed his peace." He begins to pace as he runs his ghostly fingers through his hair. I remember what that was once like, but now I know how it feels to be human again. "There's talk here on the island. Some of the other ghosts think he was banished here, that this was his prison."

If I were human and in complete control of this bodysuit, this is where I would feel goose bumps on my flesh and my hair standing on end. This isn't a ghost at all, not even close.

"Does he have a body he morphs into? Or is he just smoke and sulfur?" I inquire as I motion for the kid to follow me outside.

"He's mostly black smoke, but we've seen his face. Those of us who have been up close and personal." He kicks at the earth and gives a loud sigh, telling me I'm in for another storytime. "My best friend on this island, Jeff, and his girlfriend, Moira, were here with me at one point. Both were killed when one swing hit the donut hut they were behind and caused an explosion from the gas tank. So time here sucked, but at least I wasn't alone. Until that asshole started showing up and terrorizing everyone."

I wave my hands for him to hurry this storytime along. I'd like to still come back and wake Mary up with Connor's cock.

"Jeff was a hothead. He was easily set off, so when this thing showed up and started toying with Moira, he fought like hell. Not that it did much because it just *ate* them."

"Kid, stop saying it ate them. This wasn't a spitfire buffet. The fucking thing absorbed their energy," I exhale loudly and head for the door, having heard enough of his little story.

"Where are you going?" His scared voice trails behind me as I open the door, loving the feeling of using hands, feet, and a cock.

"I need to piss," I inform him as I shut the door on him and laugh when half his body is still on the inside. I grab Connor's cock out of his pants and aim for a bush, watching the yellow stream as if it were the most riveting movie ever. I don't want to take anything for granted, because one day I could find myself on my knees and sucking off the big daddy's burning cock in hell. "Where does this guy usually hang out?" I ask the sniveling kid as I shake off Connor's dick, the action giving me more pleasure than it should. It's astounding how much you take for granted when you're alive.

"The swing ride," he answers, his voice quivering with emotion. Honestly, these teens are so fucking hormonal.

"Hey, question. Do you go near that place knowing you single-handedly took down an entire park?" I begin to walk toward the rides as he scrambles behind me.

"That wasn't my fault!" he exclaims. "That thing did it!"

"You're like the biggest villain of all, kid. Out here making history and shit, we're more alike than you think." I chuckle as he huffs behind me. "The mystery of this island rests on your inability to work a fucking crank. How poetic."

"I'm telling you, that ride was always finicky, but that thing had plans to destroy this place, and it's been terrorizing us ever since." I know my playing on his guilt and torturing him about what happened that day has nothing on what's been terrorizing them for decades.

"It's a demon," I tell him, my voice low as I push aside some overgrown branches. "Probably a banished one. I know a little bit about them myself."

"A demon?" He mulls the word over. I glance over my shoulder to see his ghostly brows dipping over his eyes. "How do you know?"

"It sounds similar to what I've once experienced but worse. Some demons you can summon for wealth, power, and protection, and even though they are malevolent things, those have a purpose for being in our dimension. Then there are those so vile, so devious that not even the hottest depths of Hell can handle them. They're banished to different dimensions to live out an eternity of pain and loneliness. This particular demon found himself lucky and has been feasting, savoring you all as food for decades."

"No." He shakes his head. "This can't be. So are all of my friends... Did they..."

"Lost forever, I would assume." I nod and step onto the cracked concrete of the theme park grounds and look around. "But he's been weak. Human flesh is more powerful than a ghost and he's severely lacking that on this island."

"Until now."

I won't lie. His words send a chill down my spine because even though I'm not a human, I am encased in one. I tend to forget that Connor is me and I am Connor.

"He can try," I growl as I stride toward the swing ride, knowing that ground probably has his sigil burned into the earth. The only way a demon can travel or stay in a place is to be summoned by its sigil and the minute it fades, so will the demon. Here, it must be a permanent branding.

"Wait, are you going to summon it now?"

"Run along, kid. You're useless to me now," I throw over my shoulder as I stop in front of the crank, the same one I was drawn to the moment we stepped on this island.

Underneath the crank is a block of concrete, which encases a conduit for the wires to run the ride. The block is cracked and I can smell the sulfur just as strong as the first day I stood here.

"If you were to break that thing open, you would find my sigil. That's what you're looking for, no?"

I turn at the sound of the child's voice and find Andy standing there in the center of the swing ride's destruction, his hands in his pockets and an evil smirk on his face. This is the demon's earthly form, and when he hasn't been terrorizing the island in his true form, he's been walking amongst them in this one.

I toe the concrete block and watch as a chunk crumbles away. Nothing can sit on top of a sigil without eventually being destroyed.

"Why were you sent here?" The kid has his eyes on the block.

"I fucked Lilith." Andy laughs, his head tossed back. "I pissed off the wrong demon and found myself banished here."

"I'll help you return." I try a diplomatic approach. "We'll find the sigil and—"

"And what?" I turn at the sneer in the child's voice. "Send me back to Hell? I still have a century left on my sentence and I refuse to serve it here alone. Besides, now I have a few humans to feed off of. I'm saving the girl for last." Black smoke swirls around the child's body, slowly transforming it into the form I saw standing over James. Those red eyes look sinister and similar to another's I saw so very long ago. The sight has rage bubbling inside of me and I growl as I step forward. "Tell me, weak ghost, how much am I going to enjoy that little girl?" The sound of its voice has my stomach flipping and my teeth clenching together.

Mary is *my* little girl.

I want to fight it, to grab its inky smoke in between my hands and crush it, but that won't do anything to defeat it. Instead, it'll be basically handing it Connor to feed from.

"What's your name?" I ask through gritted teeth. I've never in my life possessed such self-control, both human and ghost lives combined.

"A demon's name is sacred," it replies before giving me a tsk. "But I will indulge you since these are your last few moments here on Earth. Valac is what I'm called."

Valac is a well-known demon of the underworld and I know he is deceiving and evil. There was a time in my human life when researching demons took up a lot of my time, and this one was one I had read to stay away from. To avoid at all costs. Now I see why.

I'm not stupid enough to think I can fight it, but I do carry something along with me, something that's been etched into the fabric of my soul, *someone* who has no other choice but to protect me until I no longer exist. It was a pact made long ago, and it remains whether I am a human or a ghost. No matter how much it deceived me.

I have not called upon that power since I was trapped inside Belgrove without a way to escape. That was a deadly mistake, one I paid for with my life and spirit. I vowed to never repeat it, but sometimes vows are broken, along with promises. At least this time, I won't feel bad about the outcome.

Valac rushes toward me in an enormous cloud of black, acrid smoke and I raise Connor's hand to my chest just as he wakes up inside of me.

"Conroy! What the fuck is happening? No! Not this thing again!"

"Kid," I mumble as I close my eyes. "Will you shut the fuck up and let me concentrate?

"Fuck you, Conroy!" he continues to screech like a fucking female, instantly wiping away the pride I had for him after last night. *"My friends! They'll be in danger!"*

As soon as the heat hits our skin, I begin to chant, "My body, mind, and soul are yours for the taking. Come inside and bend to my will. I need your protection with my body to fill. Zozo, I summon you. I demand you to heed the pact made in blood so very long ago."

"Zozo?" I hear Valac mutter just as his claws begin to scrape along our skin. "How can you summon Zozo?"

That's the last thing I hear as I'm shoved back and slammed into a hard surface beside a cowering Connor. Both of us are shoved aside inside Connor as his body now becomes a puppet to Zozo.

"What the fuck have you done?" he asks me, his eyes wide open. "What's happening?"

"Not sure." I shrug as I lean back and shut my eyes. "We'll wait and see."

NINE

Connor

"Who is Zozo?" I ask the murdering ghost who's sitting beside me so calmly.

"A demon who preys upon kids through an Ouija Board. Do you know what that is?" He turns to look at me.

"Of course I know what that is. Are you telling me you're a demon?" I begin to shake because everything is starting to make sense.

"No, you idiot," he breathes out, an amused look on his face. "I'm just tied to one forever."

"Why? What does that mean? And what are they doing out there?" I rapidly fire questions at him as my heart pounds. I knew Conroy was always dangerous. I could feel his maliciousness inside of me, but consorting with demons is on another level.

"When you're a kid and you feel lost, alone, and so fucking scared for your life, you'll do anything, try anything, if it means the pain will stop," he begins, his eyes dropping to look at his clasped hands. "You know about my mother from the little I've said and what you've seen yourself when my guard was down, but that's not the half of it. She was sick in the fucking head, and when she met Gary, he matched her illness with a greater one of his own. Two fucked up cunts raising a kid."

I can't completely let go of the fear I have inside of me for my friends, but he's right, there's nothing we can do about it right now. I've been wanting to know what made Conroy become the evil man he was, and now I'm getting my wish.

"My oldest memories are of my mother climbing into my bed and calling me her husband. I was still in pampers. She assured me it was normal, and all mothers touched their children the same way. Even some fathers. So to me, that was what I was supposed to endure every night at bedtime. But trust me, kid, as I got older, regardless of if she was my mother, that shit felt good." He gives me a crooked smile, his eyes shining with sincerity.

I feel light-headed and disgusted at his words. How could he enjoy such a touch from his parent?

"I can see you judging me." He nods when I don't say anything. "Hell, I get it, but even now, I get hard at the thought of fucking my mother's asshole." I slam my eyes shut to avoid seeing the pleasure in his and slap a hand over my mouth, preparing to hold back whatever may find its way upward. "I didn't know any better," he continues, and I want to scream at him to stop. I don't know how much more of this I can listen to. "I didn't go to school, and we lived in a shack in the middle of the woods. I knew no one else, nothing else but my mother. No TV, some books in which I taught myself how to read, but nothing else. Not until I was fourteen and finally ventured out of those woods. I found people, a town, and I found *him*."

"The demon?" I whisper as I wring my hands together.

"Worse." He shakes his head. "So much worse. I thought I found someone strong enough to come back and help me and Mom. Someone who would be able to feed us beyond picked berries, mushrooms, and stream water."

"Who was he?" I ask, fearful of the answer but also needing to know.

"Some homeless junkie living on the street, but to me, he looked large, strong, and capable. My mother fought him the moment she saw me with him, but she was no match, and those first few times he fucked her, she screamed and fought for me to help. Instead, I found myself watching in awe. I liked how she was being forced, and I liked that it was hurting her. Now she knew how it felt."

His eyes have a faraway look in them, and his posture is relaxed, even while he's talking about rape and child molestation. It's as if he's telling a mundane story. The whole thing is making me sick.

"Gary began to introduce her to drugs, crack, meth, and in some cases, huffing fucking cans of air. Whatever gave them the high they needed, and during their cracked-out days, they would turn on me for entertainment. Gary not only raped and fucked my mother but me as well. He especially liked when I was forced to fuck my mother and got a kick out of how much I enjoyed myself when I would come inside whichever orifice was available. I fought back, but Gary was bigger, stronger, and he began to beat me unconscious, then rape me while I was blacked out. I would wake up in agony, my insides on fire." He looks at me, a grin still lingering on his mouth, and I can't help but fear him a little more. He's also not in his right mind, and he could've very well inherited that from his mother.

"Why didn't you just run away?" I ask. "Living on the streets must've been better than that."

"No." He shakes his head. "I wanted revenge, and I discovered it in the salvation of a wooden board I found in a cupboard of the rundown shack. I took it out to the woods and sat it in front of me as I began to beg. I needed saving, and I didn't care who did it. I stabbed a sharpened branch through my palm,"—he holds up his hand, showing me a jagged, circular scar—"and I let my blood pool on the Ouija as I screamed for help."

"A blood oath," I breathe out as my chest hammers with fear. "You made a blood oath with a demon."

"Zozo came to my beck and call. He loves a child with the Ouija Board. Instead of just killing me and consuming my essence, he decided he was bored that day and wanted something different. I told him what was happening to me and what I needed, and unbeknownst to me, he had something he needed from me in return. I made a blood bond with him, tying us together for eternity."

I know the principle of a blood bond. We've read about them as Phantom Chasers preparing for the different types of paranormals we could potentially stumble upon, but I don't think any of us actually believed half of what we read. It was fun searching for ghosts and things that went bump in the night. Until now.

"Zozo asked me what my first demand would be, and I said to kill my mother and Gary. And so he did. It was in the most spectacular way, and I was ecstatic. I bet their bodies are still there inside that shack, decayed and forgotten about. I left those woods freer than I'd ever been and I soon integrated into society. I worked at a local campground as a caretaker, and after a few years, I forgot about Zozo and the pact we made, but he never forgot me."

The campground where Conroy worked was in Pensacola, this much I learned when we researched him before going to Belgrove. He was indeed a groundskeeper, and he's heading toward a story that I, and most of the people in the United States, know well.

"One summer, we had a bunch of little girls come for a camping trip, all of them dressed in little brown dresses and learning about nature. I thought that was cool, that all kids should learn how to survive in the wild. I know how well it benefited me. The first few nights were fine, no trouble came from those four cabins of children, until the third night. One of those girls brought a Ouija Board with them, and it was like a beacon for Zozo. I remember falling asleep in my bed and then waking up in the middle of the woods with blood all over my naked body."

"You weren't the one who hurt those girls." My breath leaves me in a rush as I stare at the man who looks like the Devil incarnate.

"No, I didn't. Not that anyone believed me. I tried to blame it on the demon I made a pact with. I tried to tell them it was the Ouija Board that summoned him, but in the end, I was deemed a schizophrenic and tossed into Belgrove. I had also learned it wasn't the first time Zozo took over my body to commit crimes without my knowledge, and I had a laundry list of child rape behind me. The one thing I despised."

"But you said you enjoyed children back at Belgrove," I dispute. "I remember."

He laughs as he shrugs his shoulders. "When people refuse to hear your pleas, you either fight until you die, or join them. I always did like the easy way out, hence why I summoned a demon in the first place."

I can see why people had a hard time believing him, especially back during a time when technology provided no clues about the spirit world or what lurks on the other side. Ghosts and demons were used as fear tactics but didn't actually exist.

"What happened at Belgrove?" I ask him, unsure of why I want to keep this story going, but knowing I need all the answers now. I want to know about the ghost who inhabits my body.

"I wanted out of there. Obviously, they hated me because I was a kiddie fucker or whatever. I was beaten every day, force-fed scraps from the kitchen, and…" He takes a breath, swallowing down the fear I hear mounting in his voice. "I was experimented on. Three nights of electroshock, waterboarding, and then the final straw was when they said they planned to castrate me. They wanted to see if these balls"—he grips his cock in his hand—"were the reason why I wanted to hurt little girls. I panicked, and that night in bed, I summoned him. He was my last resort."

"He didn't work out for you then. What the fuck makes you think he'll do it for you now?" I huff. "You were locked inside that room to die a slow, painful death because of him."

"But I still got these balls, kid." He looks at me with a large smile, his eyes filled with mirth, and I can't help it. I chuckle at him. Conroy has had a terrible life and had no one to help him. It makes me feel bad for the guy.

"Do you think Zozo will win? Will we get off this island?" I ask him.

"Zozo is a fucked-up bird. He'll get us out of here," he says with conviction. "I just don't know what the consequences will be."

My body feels as though it was put through the spin cycle inside the washing machine. Everything hurts and my head feels heavy as I open my eyes to look at my surroundings. I'm lying on my back in the center of the park, and all I smell is the sulfuric stench of the demon. The sky is beginning to lighten with the dawn, but the stars are still visible, telling me it'll be a clear day.

As I slowly sit up, I'm becoming clearer and two things stand out to me. I'm still alive and in my body, and the demon—both demons—seem to be gone.

"You did it." I turn at the sound of a voice and see Danny standing a few feet away from me, his eyes wide and his hands trembling. "You fought that thing and you won."

"It wasn't me," I tell him as I scrub a hand down my face.

Just then a sharp bark fills the air and Jane comes bounding out of some bushes toward me. Her fur is matted and wet and has leaves nestled in the coarse fur, but she looks fearful and excited at the same time.

"She watched the fight and was whining from behind the bushes," Danny tells me as she jumps into my lap and licks my face. "All of us watched."

I can feel eyes on me, but I can't see anyone besides Danny. "My friends?" I ask him as I stagger to my feet.

"Still sleeping in the cabin. I can't believe that thing was Andy all along, and you vanquished him." He looks at me with awe, as if I'm his savior, and I'm hit with a sudden panic.

"You can't tell James about this," I beg. "My friends can't know about…" My hands press into my chest.

"I know." He nods. "I won't say anything about it. I just want to get off this island… We all do."

"And don't tell him about Andy, about what he was, or what happened here," I demand.

"I won't." He shakes his head and relief washes over me as I look around.

The Park is even more destroyed and now there are charred and burning trees mixed in with the destruction. "What happened?"

"You turned into red smoke, and your voice sounded mechanical, like a robot. At first, you were speaking to one another in a language I didn't understand, but then that thing began to get hostile. Suddenly it was a clashing of red and black and the sounds were like nothing I had ever heard. Screeching metal and grinding gears. It was awful. And the smell…" His nose crinkles with the memory as I nod, thankful that Conroy was here inside of me to face that thing. Surely we would have died here on this island without him.

Wait. I still and search inside of me for the man I have despised until mere hours ago. It's been silent and I'm feeling empty, like I'm missing a part of myself.

"Conroy?" I shriek internally as my hands grow slick with sweat and my breathing begins to falter. *"Conroy! Are you here?"*

104

"*Yeah, kid.*" he sounds tired, drained of energy, and he's lacking his smartass remarks. *"It's a give-and-take whenever I call him. He takes a bit of me each time."*

"Okay, rest," I tell him and then motion for Danny to follow me back to the cabin. "Ghosts linger because they have unfinished business or they don't know they're dead. What are we working with here on the island? A mix of that or all unfinished business?"

"Both. Mostly the children don't understand they're dead." He runs his fingers through his hair. "But I can remedy that. I'll gather everyone and explain what happened and what they are, but some of us are lingering because we are hoping for justice." He stops walking and looks around. "We were forced to stay trapped here, but even if that thing wasn't here to terrorize us, it would be the same. We want to see justice and can't move on without it."

"What if I promise to leak this all to the press, to let them know of the true horrors that happened here and exactly why they did. We have your work papers with us, we could give that to the media. They would know who the investors were on this island." I pray it's enough to help these people find peace and to move on.

After a few moments of silence, Danny nods and I feel the relief all the way to my bones. I'm weary and sore, and just want off this dreaded island. "That will work for most."

"For most?" I inquire, my head tipping to the side. "I don't have much more to offer."

"Let's go wake up your friends and talk." He walks ahead of me toward the cabin and I find myself too tired to argue.

James

"He says if we promise to expose what we learned here on the island, we would help many cross over," I repeat Danny's words to the others sitting on our makeshift bed.

I was woken by Connor coming into the cabin early this morning, looking disheveled and wary. He told me he had been taking a piss when the bushes rattled and scared him half to death. Then I saw Danny behind him.

Now we're here, trying to figure out what we can do to help the ghosts here.

"But what about that thing?" Nick asks. "The thing that attacked you last night?"

My body throbs with pain at the mention of my ordeal, and I swallow down the lingering fear. I don't want to face it again.

"It's gone," Danny states, a smile lighting up his face. "I think it realized you guys can't be messed with."

"He says it's gone. That it left," I inform everyone as a relieved sigh spills from my mouth.

"Well, I think we could collectively promise to expose this island and the people who created it," Nick suggests, and the rest of us agree.

Danny's face lights up and he pokes his head out of the door, a laugh escaping his mouth. "They're all leaving!"

"They're crossing over," I tell the others.

"Wait!" Nick exclaims and jumps up from the bed. "I want to say goodbye to Andy."

"Tell him he's already gone!" Danny exclaims, and I don't miss the frantic look on his face.

"He's passed, Nicky." I drop my hand to his shoulder as he slumps. "That's a good thing."

"Yeah, it is," he mumbles. "I just wanted to say bye."

Connor comes up behind him and wraps his arms around his waist, resting his chin on Nick's shoulder. "Come sit down and let's hear what we gotta do before we can leave this place."

I like that they've figured their shit out. It's less stressful on the group and when I look at Mary, I can see the relief on her face as well. Now, we're really a team.

"Danny is still here," I remark as the ghost slowly turns back around to face us. "Why haven't you left?" I ask him.

"Because I need something a little more," he admits with a sheepish smile. Jane picks that moment to cross the room and sniff the floor at his feet before settling on the spot he's standing. Almost as if she knows he's there.

"Danny needs a little more to cross over." I look over my shoulder at the others, making sure they agree to such a thing before I ask him to carry on.

They all nod in unison, and pride hits me square in the chest. We really are out here making a difference in the world.

"Okay," I nod to the kid. "Tell us what you need."

"My mother and sister must be haunted by the thought of me dying here and unable to know why or how. If they're still living, I want them to know what happened to me. You have my address there,"—he nods to his suitcase—"please find them."

"He wants us to find his mother and sister and tell them what happened to him here on the island." I turn around again to find Mary standing from the cot and coming to stand beside me.

"I think I would be honored to do that," she says with a smile.

"We all would," Connor adds.

I turn back to Danny, my heart squeezing at the hopeful look in his eyes. "We promise to find your family and let them know."

His smile grows huge on his face as his eyes widen. He looks to the sky and I notice he begins to slowly fade. "Thank you, James." Then I swear he nods in the direction of Nick and Connor as he completely disappears.

"He's gone." I turn and gather Mary in my arms as I look at my brother and Connor, both of them sitting on the bed and holding hands. "Let's get out of this fucking place."

Jane jumps up with a bark and runs to Connor, nuzzling his hand with her snout. Even the dog is fed up with this place.

EPILOGUE
Mary

I made it off of Silent Night Island Resort in one piece and in better spirits than when I arrived. Connor and Nick have sorted through their issues and we're stronger now, my three boyfriends and me.

Weird, right? I know. Three boyfriends. But each of them gives me something I need, and I hope, in turn, I complete a part of them too. It's been working out well, and we've hit no bumps in the road.

"I can't believe they still live here," James murmurs beside me as we stop at the bottom of a driveway to stare up at a small bungalow.

"I'm glad they do. It made this a whole lot easier," I muse as he grabs my hand to lead me toward the front door.

There's an older model Ford truck sitting in the driveway and the lawns are a little overgrown, but otherwise, it's a normal-looking house.

We stand on the porch and James gives me a look, his sexy mouth curving into a grin. "Are you ready?"

"As I'll ever be," I reply as I grip the envelope in my hand a little tighter.

James rings the doorbell and I wait for any sound to tell us someone is home. Finally, the sound of shuffling feet nears the door, and I squeeze James' hand. The locks are turned and when the door slowly swings forward, we come face-to-face with an older lady, her face lined with deep wrinkles.

RENE & BROOKS

"Can I help you?" Her voice shakes with age.

"My name is James and this is Mary," James answers. "We're here to speak to you about your son."

"Danny?" Her eyes widen as she looks back and forth between us. "You're a little too young to have known my son."

"Ma!" a woman's voice calls from inside the house. "Who are you talking to?"

"There are some young folk out here saying they want to talk about Danny!" she yells out.

"No!" A woman appears behind the old lady. "No press. It's been ages. Why are you all sniffing around now?"

"We're not the press," I assure her. "We have information on the people responsible for Danny's death. Could we come inside?"

"No one can access that information," the younger woman sneers. "What game is this?"

"Are you Christine?" James asks as the woman gasps.

"How would you know that?" she whispers as her hand shakily covers her mouth.

"We're not lying when we say we have information, and we would like to come inside to speak with you."

"Oh, move, Christine. Let them in, they're just children," Danny's mother shoos her back. "Come in. We would love to hear about my son's disappearance on that island."

I don't miss that she says disappearance and not death.

We're led into the living room as Christine continues to stare at us with a shocked expression. "There's no way you're old enough to know Danny."

"No, but we recently ventured onto Silent Night Island," I explain as we sit on the couch. "Of course it was illegal, but we took a chance that the place isn't heavily monitored anymore and we were right. We found the cabin your son was staying in and we came across his paperwork for the job." I hand Christine the envelope as I continue to look into Danny's mother's eyes. They're beginning to mist the more we speak about him. "These are a copy, of course, and another copy has

110

been sent to a few news outlets. We've been told the story will be aired in the next few days."

"In that envelope, there are names of investors and other places they owned," James takes over as Christine pulls out the papers. Her eyes scan over the pages as tears stream down her cheeks. "There was this as well." James stands up and hands her the photos we found in Danny's cabin. "It was evident he cared about his family and we thought it would only be right to bring these to you."

"Thank you," she whispers as tears drip from her jaw. "Ma!" she exclaims as her eyes go back to the paper in her hand. "This same company owns Lovers Cove Getaway. That was the place you and Dad went!"

"You've been there?" James leans forward, eager for the story.

"I lost my husband there," is Danny's mother's reply.

ALSO BY

STORY BROOKS

Scan the QR Code below for more details!

ABOUT THE AUTHOR

Story Brooks, also known as Cat Vann, lives in South Carolina with her husband, three kids, and plenty of animals running about.

Story has always been a reader first and dedicated book worm. She loves connecting with other readers and authors in the book world and discovering new inspiration to fuel her passion of writing.

ALSO BY C.A. RENE

Scan the QR Code below for more details!

ABOUT C.A. RENE

C.A. Rene lives in Toronto, Canada with her family, where most of the year varies from chilly to frigid. Most days you'll find her wrapped in her many blankets in bed while reading or writing her next dark, twisted story.

Her stories boast of inclusivity and refusal to be conformed in any small box. Writing across genres is a hobby and drinking wine is a must… Or coffee … with a splash of Baileys.